Witch Is When
I Said Goodbye

Published by Implode Publishing Ltd
© Implode Publishing Ltd 2016

Chapter 1

After Jack Maxwell's transfer had been cancelled, I thought he and I had finally made a real connection, and that our next date would be something special — a kind of new beginning. The kind of date where the sky is blue, birds are singing and cute little bunny rabbits hop happily around.

The reality was more: rain clouds, vultures overhead and a boiled rabbit.

The evening had been overshadowed by his suspension, and although he made the effort, I could see it was playing heavily on his mind. I'd promised myself I wouldn't raise the subject because I knew he didn't want to talk about it, but in the end I had to say something.

"So, what's happening with the internal investigation?" Oh boy, I made it sound like an endoscopy.

"Internal Affairs have interviewed me." He sighed. "But I haven't heard anything back from them yet."

"Come on, Jack. That's ridiculous. This should've been cleared up in a matter of days. Why is it dragging on like this?"

"You don't understand how the system works. The cogs turn very slowly."

"What are you doing to speed things along? You can't just lie back and let them treat you like this." Again, with the endoscopy.

"They have procedures to follow."

"Why are you being so reasonable?"

"Getting angry won't do any good."

It seemed to work for me.

"Why won't you at least allow me to help?"

"No! I've told you. You need to stay out of this."

The man was exasperating. Why couldn't he be more reasonable? Like — err — well, like me, for example.

We cut the evening short. When he dropped me back at my place, I didn't invite him in; neither of us was in the right frame of mind. He was angry with me for trying to stick my oar in, and I was angry with him for not being angry enough.

"I'll call you," he said, as I climbed out of his car.

I thought about apologising, but then I thought about custard creams instead.

"Yeah. Okay. See you."

And then he drove off. Another in a long line of successful dates. Would I ever learn to keep my big mouth shut? Answers on a postcard to: Not a chance, c/o never going to happen.

***

The next morning, I was still in a foul mood. So much for fluffy bunnies and our 'new start'. It was all Winky's fault.

Why? I don't know why, but I had to blame someone, and you didn't think it was going to be me, did you?

If I'd drawn up a list of three people I didn't want to bump into that morning, it would have been: TDO, Grandma, and — too late! There he was.

"Good morning, Jill," Mr Ivers said.

"Morning." I couldn't bring myself to say 'good'.

If he said the word 'movie' in the next thirty seconds, I would be forced to end him — I'd do it humanely, obviously. I'm not totally without compassion.

"What do you think to her?" he gushed.

I wasn't in the mood for cryptic puzzles. 'Her' could have been anything from some movie 'goddess' I'd never heard of, right through to his pet terrapin.

"You're going to have to give me more than that. Who's 'her'?"

"My new car of course!"

"Where is it?" There was no bubble car or three-wheeler anywhere to be seen.

"There!"

I still couldn't see it. Unless it was parked behind the red, open-top sports car. A Diamond, if I wasn't mistaken—one of my favourite cars. I couldn't have cared less about the Iversmobile, but I *did* want a closer look at this beauty.

"So, what do you think?" Mr Ivers had followed me.

"Where is it?"

"There! Right in front of you!"

"This?"

"Yes."

"Is yours?"

"Yes."

"The Diamond?"

"Yes."

"Did you hire it?" I knew there were companies which specialised in hiring out top-end cars like this for the day. I'd actually considered hiring a Diamond myself, but it would have cost me a bag full of gold and the promise of my first-born.

"No. I bought it."

I was missing something here. What was it that Mr Ivers did for a living? I had no idea; I'd never cared enough to ask. He'd never struck me as a drug dealer or city trader, so how else could he have afforded it?

"Did you win the lottery?"

"Never do it. I don't believe in gambling."

"Come into an inheritance?"

"Nothing like that. I got a great deal on this little beauty. It was a real steal."

"You stole it?"

"No, of course not." He laughed. "All the paperwork is in order. Checked and double-checked. It's all a question of having the right contacts. I bought it from another film buff, who I met through my column in The Bugle. When he told me how much he wanted, I snatched his hand off."

I ran my fingers along the smooth lines of the bonnet. I never thought I'd say this, but I was actually a little jealous of Mr Ivers. I could just picture myself behind the wheel of a Diamond. Being a witch had its perks, but how come I couldn't magic myself a car like this? What better, selfless use of magic could there be?

"Have you taken her for a spin, yet?"

"Not yet. It was only delivered late last night. I thought I might put her through her paces this evening. You can join me, if you like?"

What a quandary!

Pro: I get to ride in the most beautiful car in the world.

Con: Mr Ivers.

Pro: Maybe I'd get to take the wheel for a while.

Con: Mr Ivers.

It was a difficult decision, and all hinged on whether or not I'd get to have a turn at the wheel. To do that, I'd have to use all my womanly wiles, and flirt with Mr Ivers. But that would be totally unethical as I had no real interest in the man at all.

"I'd love to join you."

What? Judge me all you like.

"Great! We can drive to the coast, and along the coast road if the weather's still fine."

"Sounds great."

***

"There's something going on with that cat, again," Mrs V said when I walked into the office.

"What's he up to now?"

"I don't know, but there's an awful lot of meowing coming from your office."

By now, you might have thought that nothing Winky could do would surprise me, but somehow that little bundle of furry joy still managed it.

He was perched on the windowsill—holding his two little flags. Facing him were eight other cats. Eight! They were watching him so intently they barely registered my arrival. Winky was something of a master when it came to semaphore. He'd originally used it to communicate with Bella, his girlfriend, the feline supermodel. From there, they'd progressed to sending messages via remote control helicopter, and then via smartphones. But Winky still had a soft spot for his little flags, and if I'm honest, so did I. It was such an unusual, and yet endearing conduit for romance.

But why had he chosen to bring the flags out again, and more importantly, why were there so many other cats in the office?

"Do you mind?" He shot me a one-eyed glare. "You're

interrupting my lesson."

"I'm doing what?"

"Lesson? Interrupting it? What's not to understand?"

"What kind of lesson?"

He sighed—obviously exasperated. "I'll give you a clue." He waved his flags around. "Care to take a wild guess?"

"You're giving semaphore lessons?"

"Once again, you demonstrate why you are a member of the private investigator elite." He turned back to the class. "Take five, guys, while I give my human a clue. It seems she's all out of them."

The other cats began to practise their semaphore while Winky came over to talk to me.

"Couldn't you have waited outside until the lesson had ended?"

"No, I couldn't. In case you hadn't noticed, this is my office. And anyway, I'm surprised there's a demand for semaphore lessons."

"I might have had something to do with that."

"I should have known."

"It all started with a post I made on FelineSocial a few days ago. I just happened to mention how Bella and I first got together. I only did it as a sort of feline-interest story, but after it appeared, I was contacted by lots of cats who are in the same position as I was. They have a love interest close by, but don't have access to either a remote control helicopter or a smartphone. Semaphore offers them the ideal solution."

"But if they don't have a smartphone, how did they even see your post on FelineSocial?"

"That's a very astute question. We'll make a P.I. of you

yet. Most of them are able to access one of their human's smartphones, tablets or computers for a few minutes here and there. But not long enough or often enough to sustain a meaningful relationship. Once they've completed this course, they'll be able to use semaphore whenever they like."

"Where on earth did they all get their flags from?"

He grinned.

I should have known. "You're selling flags too?"

"Of course. I couldn't let a golden opportunity like that pass me by."

"And robbing them blind, no doubt."

"Shush!! He glanced around to make sure the other cats weren't listening, but they were too busy practising. "If they buy the flags at the same time as they book the lesson, I give them a twenty-five per cent discount. I can't be more generous than that."

"Twenty-five per cent discount on how much?"

"Twenty pounds."

"Twenty pounds for a couple of flags which you could get for fifty-pence at the seaside?"

"Thirty."

"Thirty what?"

"Two of these flags cost thirty pence at the seaside. Where do you think I got them from?"

"That's an outrageous mark-up."

"I don't see anyone complaining. Anyway, you're missing the point. They're not paying for the flags; they're paying for a new way to communicate with their loved ones."

"And how much do you charge for the lessons?"

"Sixty pounds."

"Sixty?" I was clearly in the wrong business. "Where do they get the money from?"

"We cats have our methods."

Their poor owners were no doubt going to find some strange charges on their next credit card bills.

"When will you be done in here?"

"We're almost done for today, but this is only the first of many classes. There's a waiting list."

"What about *my* business? What am I supposed to tell my clients?"

"I can teach your clients semaphore too, if you like. I'll even give them a discount."

"I meant, how can I bring clients into the office when you and your friends here are busy waving flags around?"

"If and when you ever get a client, we can worry about that then. But, I won't hold my breath."

"If you're going to use my office, I think that I should get a cut of the money you're making."

"Okay. I can live with that. And besides, I did promise these guys that they'd get complimentary food and drink included in the course. So, I'll need you to buy more milk and salmon."

"Do what?"

"Possibly a little tuna as an alternative?"

"Hold on, I didn't say anything about buying extra food and drink for your students."

"I'll be prepared to give you a generous share of the takings."

"Fifty/fifty."

"Eighty/twenty."

"Sixty/forty."

"Seventy/thirty."

"Sixty-five/thirty-five."

"Okay, but you'd better hurry up with the milk because this is thirsty work. Full cream, obviously."

"Obviously."

***

I had such mixed emotions. On the one hand, I was about to go for a drive in my all-time favourite car, the Diamond. On the other hand —

"Evening, Jill. Are you ready for a spin in this old girl?"

Mr Ivers was wearing plus-fours, which did nothing for him. He didn't have the legs for them. I'd gone for a sixties-style outfit. With my hair in a ponytail, and sunglasses, I had more than a touch of the Hepburn going on. I oozed class and sophistication. As always.

"Yeah, I'm looking forward to the drive." If not the company.

"Off we go!" he whooped. "We'll take the motorway to the coast, and then we'll take the coastal roads. The sea breeze will be great with the top down."

"Sounds fantastic."

It really did, but I should have known it was too good to be true.

Why were we going so slowly? The speedometer had barely moved. Perhaps he was just being overly cautious as this was his first time out in the Diamond. Once we were on the motorway, I felt sure he would open her up.

But he didn't. We were still moving at a snail's pace.

"What's wrong? Are you stuck in first gear?"

"I don't know. I'm in top gear, and I've got my foot to the floor. I think there must be something wrong with her."

He pulled off the motorway onto an A-road. Moments later, a moped overtook us. It was so embarrassing.

"There's obviously something wrong, Mr Ivers. Do you have roadside assistance?"

"Yes, I've been a member for years."

"You'd better pull into that layby and give them a call."

We had to wait almost two hours for roadside assistance to arrive. Still, it wasn't all bad. Mr Ivers passed the time by providing me with a detailed run-down of all the movies he'd seen that month. Yawn!

By the time the mechanic arrived, I was practically comatose.

"Hello there, you two." The mechanic had a smudge of oil on his nose, and two missing front teeth. "Beautiful motor. What seems to be the problem?"

"I've no idea." Mr Ivers shrugged. "I've only just bought her. This is the first time I've taken her for a spin."

"Okay. Pop the bonnet and I'll take a look."

The man disappeared under the bonnet, but only for a few seconds. When he stood up again, he had a puzzled look on his face. I had a horrible feeling this wasn't going to be good news.

"You say you've only recently acquired the car?"

"Yes."

"Did you pay much for it?"

"No, it was a steal. A real bargain."

"That would explain it."

"What's wrong?" I interrupted.

"It's the engine."

"Has it blown?"

"No, it's still working fine."

"Then why are we going so slowly?"

"It's not the right one."

This man was beginning to annoy me. "Right one for what?"

"This car. I normally see these engines under the bonnets of much smaller cars."

"How small?"

"Bubble car small."

Oh bum!

I've never been so embarrassed in all my life. As we crawled back home, we were overtaken by a couple on a tandem. It was almost midnight by the time we got back to the flat.

"Sorry about tonight, Jill." Mr Ivers helped me out of the car. "I never thought to look at the engine."

Why would he? It was such an inconsequential part of the car.

I somehow forced a smile. It was either that or strangle him.

"Maybe we can try again when I can afford to buy the correct engine."

"Yeah, maybe." There was more chance of me being signed to Formula One than taking another ride with Mr Ivers.

Chapter 2

The next morning, I was still having flashbacks about the previous evening's events. The only saving grace was that no one I knew had witnessed my humiliation. If Kathy ever found out, I'd never hear the end of it.

Winky was on my computer—yet again! He was laughing hysterically at something.

"Have you ever thought of getting your own YouTube channel?" he said when he'd eventually managed to compose himself.

"What are you talking about?"

"You really should set one up. If you monetise it, you'll probably make more money than you do with this P.I. gig."

"I don't have time for your cryptic mind games. What are you talking about?"

"This!" He pointed to the screen.

Oh no! The video showed a tandem overtaking an open-top sports car—a Diamond.

"Recognise anyone?" He chuckled.

"No."

"Not even the woman in the headscarf and sunglasses?"

"I especially don't recognise her."

Thank goodness I'd worn those; no one could ever prove it was me.

"That's not you then?"

"Definitely not—"

Then, the woman in the video removed her sunglasses, and turned her head to one side. It was obvious to anyone watching that it was me.

"You're a natural." Winky paused the video. "First, the

video outside the London premiere, and now this one. If you could knock one of these out each week, you'd be making bank. Even after my cut."

"Your cut? For doing what exactly?"

"Setting up your channel. Editing and uploading the videos. Promotion via social media. There's a lot of work involved in being a YouTube celebrity."

"You can forget it. I'm not making a fool of myself just to earn a few pounds."

"Why not? You're already doing it for free."

I looked around for something to throw at him, but he'd read my mood, and disappeared under the sofa.

Winky was still hiding when Mrs V came charging into the office. It was obvious that something was seriously wrong.

"Whatever's the matter Mrs V?" I'd never seen her look so upset.

"It's terrible, Jill. Just terrible. One of the members of our knitting circle, Cecelia Longbourn, has been murdered."

"What happened?"

"Her daughter, Jessie White, rang me just now. Apparently she found her mother's body yesterday evening. The police have been questioning Jessie for most of the night."

"Would you like to go home? I can give you a lift."

"No. I'm all right. I'd rather stay here. I don't want to be alone in the house."

Just then, the phone in the outer office rang.

"It's probably Jessie again."

Mrs V rushed to answer it; I followed. As she listened,

the colour began to drain from her face, and her hands began to shake.

"Was that Jessie again?" I asked, as soon as she'd finished on the call.

"No." She slumped down in her chair.

"What is it?"

"It's happened again. Another member of the knitting circle, Rowena Crowsfoot, has been murdered too. Her husband found her last night."

No wonder Mrs V was in shock. "Would you like a glass of water? Or some tea?"

"No. I'll be okay. I just need a minute. You have to help, Jill. You have to find out who did this."

"Of course I will. Do you think Jessie White will talk to me?"

"I'll give her a call." Mrs V's hands were still shaking as she held the phone. "Jessie. It's Annabel Versailles. Yes. Look, I'm sorry to have to tell you this, but Rowena Crowsfoot has also been found murdered. Yes, it's terrible. My boss, Jill Gooder, is a private investigator. She might be able to help. Would you be up to speaking to her? You would? Right. She'll be with you shortly."

When she'd finished on the call, Mrs V scribbled down Cecelia Longbourn's address, and handed it to me.

"I'll get straight over there, but I wish you'd let me run you home first."

"I'll be fine. Please just go and see Jessie."

***

Just as I'd expected, there were police cars parked all along the road where Cecelia Longbourn lived. The policeman on the gate was picking his nose.

"You can't go in there." He managed to extract his finger from his nasal passage just long enough to block my way.

"I'm expected."

"By who?"

"It's alright," a female voice shouted. "She's my friend."

The policeman reluctantly allowed me through, and then went back to picking his nose.

"Annabel said you were coming over," Jessie White said, once we were in the house. "I'm Jessie."

"I'm very sorry for your loss."

"Poor Mum. She didn't deserve this."

"Can you talk me through exactly what happened last night?"

"I live close by; just two streets away." She was struggling to hold it together. "I call in every night at about eight o'clock—just to make sure everything's okay. I'm usually only here for about ten or fifteen minutes, but when I came around last night—" She began to sob.

"It's okay." I put my hand on hers. "Take your time."

It took Jessie a few minutes to compose herself. "When I came around last night, I found Mum in her favourite chair. There was a knitting needle—" she took a deep breath. "There was a knitting needle in her chest."

"I'm so sorry for asking you to relive this."

"If it helps to find who did it, I don't mind."

"Did you notice anything else unusual? Anything out of place?"

"I found a typewritten note on the table next to her. It was partly in English, and partly in French. It said: 'knit une, kill une'. The police have taken it away as evidence."

Just then, Tom Hawk walked into the room. He was

Maxwell's second in command, and was presumably standing in for Jack, while he was suspended.

"Jill. Would you mind stepping outside for a minute?" He gestured for me to follow him. He didn't look happy.

"Jack warned me that you had a habit of turning up in the middle of his investigations."

"The victim was a member of my P.A.'s knitting circle."

"Who's your P.A?"

"Mrs V. I mean, Annabel Versailles. She asked me to help."

"We don't need any help."

That would be a first.

"We're perfectly capable of handling this."

"I'm sure you are. I have absolute faith in the Washbridge Police." Flattery will get you anywhere or so I'd heard. "I hear there's been a second murder."

"Your grapevine is clearly very good. Jack said he thought you had a source in the force."

"Source in the force? Jack does seem to have a bee in his bonnet about that. I can't think why. So what can you tell me about the second murder?"

"I can't tell you anything."

"I hear the MO is the same."

"How did you know—ah, I get it. You're good, Jill, I'll give you that."

"A knitting needle through the heart?"

"I can neither confirm or deny that."

"I'll take that as a 'yes'. Was there a note there too? Jessie told me she found one next to her mother."

He hesitated for a moment. "Yes, there was an identical note. I'm only telling you that because there's a chance the other members of the knitting circle may be in danger.

We're going to post an officer at the home of each of the other members—just for a few days until we know what's going on. Look, I have to get on. It's time you were leaving."

"Of course. I'll just say goodbye to Jessie."

"You're pushing your luck."

"It will only take a minute."

"Okay, but be quick."

Jessie still looked shell-shocked when I went back into the living room.

"It looks as though your mother's murder, and that of Rowena *are* connected. Can you think of any reason why someone might have wanted to kill your mother?"

"None at all. She was a darling. I can't imagine why anyone would want to hurt her. And poor Rowena. Mum and my late father were friends with her and her husband."

"I'd better be off before they throw me out." I gave her my card. "Call me if you think of anything else. Anything at all."

***

I called in at Ever A Wool Moment on my way back to the office.

"You look flustered." Kathy greeted me from behind the counter.

"I'm investigating a double murder. Two members of Mrs V's knitting circle are dead."

"Cripes! Is she okay?"

"A bit shook up, but otherwise yes."

"Any leads yet?"

"You mustn't repeat anything I tell you."

"When do I ever?"

"All the time."

"I won't this time. I promise."

"It looks like the two murders were carried out by the same man. Or woman. The victims were both stabbed with a knitting needle."

"How horrible." She glanced at the shelves which were full of potential murder weapons.

"Anyway, let's talk about something a little less gruesome. Where's Grandma?"

"I thought you said we were going to talk about something less gruesome?"

We both laughed.

"She's not in yet. I'm glad because she was in a foul mood yesterday."

"What for this time?"

"Didn't you notice the shop across the road?"

The unit directly opposite had been empty for quite some time, but there was now a new sign which read: 'Best Wool - Longer Than Ever'.

"Another wool shop? Oh dear."

"I'm surprised you haven't heard the rumblings already. Your grandmother is not a happy bunny."

"I'll bet." I laughed.

"If she catches you laughing, she'll skin you alive. She's beside herself with anger."

"What's with the tag line: Longer than Ever? Do you think they're trying to take on Everlasting Wool?"

"It sounds like it. You should go over there and take a look."

"Okay, I will."

They were still in the process of fitting out the shop. One of the posters in the window was promoting their wool subscription service: 'Never-ending Wool', which they claimed lasted *'longer than ever'*. A not too subtle dig, if ever I'd seen one. A second poster was for 'Wonder Needles', which could adjust size as required. Now where had I heard that before? Best Wool clearly planned to take the fight to 'Ever'. This was not going to go down well with Grandma.

I spotted a young woman inside the shop; she was filling the shelves that had already been installed. When I knocked on the window, she shook her head to indicate that they weren't open. I knocked again, and she eventually came to the door.

"We're not open yet." She had an accent that I couldn't place. Geordie perhaps? "We'll be open the day after tomorrow."

"Are you by any chance the owner?"

"Me?" She laughed. "No, I just work here."

"Could I speak to the owner?"

"I don't know who the owners are. I was recruited through an agency. They interviewed me, and told me to report here. I was left a list of things to do before the big opening day."

"So you don't have any idea who your boss is?"

"None. I think there must be two of them because on all the paperwork they're just referred to as M and M."

"I see. Okay, well thanks. Good luck with your new job."

I hurried across the road to report back to Kathy. "They've got wool on subscription, and 'Wonder

Needles' — and they're both cheaper than yours."

"I know. Your grandmother is absolutely furious. She's been trying to find out who the owner is, but she's drawn a blank so far."

I shouldn't have found any of this amusing, but I couldn't help it. It was good to see Grandma on the back foot for once.

"Oh, by the way." Kathy's expression changed. She had her 'Jill's in trouble' face on. "I've got a bone to pick with you."

"Isn't that my line?"

"Guess how many times I've had to take Mikey to Coffee Triangle?"

"The coffee's really good in there."

"Guess!"

"And the muffins."

"Guess!"

"Is it more than once?"

"Every time it's drum day. He doesn't let up until we take him."

"And you blame me for that?"

"Who else? You were the one who took him there in the first place."

"Things didn't exactly work out the way I'd hoped."

"No kidding."

"Are you going to let him have a drum set?"

"Pete says we should. He thinks it's a good thing that Mikey has developed an interest in music."

"Won't it drive you mad?"

"We're going to strike a deal with Mikey. We'll buy him a drum kit for his birthday, but only on the condition that he plays it in the shop where we bought it."

"How does that work?"

"They have a room upstairs that they use specifically for drums. According to the shop owner, a lot of people keep their drum kits there because, unsurprisingly, drums tend not to go down well with the neighbours. They can play them as often as they like for a nominal fee each month."

"So, Mikey would never actually bring the drum kit home?"

"That's right."

"I'm not sure he'll go for that."

"He will if it's that or no drum kit. Pete and I talked it over, and we'd rather take him there a couple of times a week, than have to listen to it all day, every day, in the house."

"What about drum day at Coffee Triangle?"

"That would be part of the deal too. No more drum day."

"Sounds like you've given it a lot of thought."

"We had to. We can't carry on with the constant drumming in the house any longer. It's bad enough with the one he's got. If he brought a full drum kit home, I'd be moving out. Or Pete would."

"Can you afford all of this?"

"The drum kit is quite expensive, but Pete still has some money left over from what the colonel left him. Without that, there's no way we could have afforded it."

"The colonel will be pleased to know that the money has been put to good use."

"What do you mean? *Will* be pleased to know? He's dead. Have you forgotten."

Whoops!

"I meant he *would* have been pleased to know. Obviously."

Chapter 3

I was on my way to speak to Rowena Crowsfoot's husband, Arnold. Mrs V had been in touch with him, and he'd agreed to see me.

His house was on the same estate as Cecelia Longbourn's. A modest two-bedroom semi-detached; its garden put the others in the street to shame. Someone clearly had green fingers.

The policeman on the gate wasn't picking his nose; he was too busy scratching his backside. Boredom did strange things to people.

"You can't go in there." You'd have thought he'd have the common courtesy to stop scratching while he spoke to me. But no.

"I'm expected."

"This is a crime scene. Move along."

"I'm expecting her," an elderly man shouted from the doorway. "She's a friend."

Scratching boy scowled, but allowed me through. I gave him a wide berth just in case whatever he had was contagious.

"Thanks for seeing me, Mr Crowsfoot."

Although he was getting on in years, he was still in remarkably good shape.

"Arnold, please."

"I'm sorry for your loss, Arnold."

"I still can't believe it. That she's gone, I mean. I keep expecting her to walk in with a cup of tea in her hand. Who would do such a thing?"

There were no words I could say that would comfort him, so I waited until he continued.

"Annabel said you're a private investigator." He looked me up and down. "Isn't that rather dangerous for a woman?"

"It can be, but I've been doing it for a long time. My father taught me everything I know."

"Ah, I see. Annabel said you might be able to find out who did this terrible thing, but what can you do that the police can't?"

"Maybe nothing, but it can't do any harm for me to try, as long as you don't object?"

"I suppose not."

"Can you talk me through what happened last night?"

"I'll try, but it's all a bit hazy."

"Take your time. There's no hurry."

"I work security now at the local history museum—on the late shift. I'm just the night watchman really. No one is ever going to break in—there's nothing of any real value worth stealing. I never get home until the early hours of the morning. That's when I found Rowena."

"I believe there was a note?"

"That's right. It didn't make any sense to me. The policeman said part of it was in French."

"Did it say something like: *'knit une, kill une'*?"

"Yes. That was it."

"Was there any sign of a break-in or a struggle?"

"Not that I could see."

"Is there anyone you can think of who might have wanted to hurt your wife? Anyone at all?"

"No one. If you'd known Rowena, you'd understand. She's such a friendly soul. She doesn't have an enemy in the world. The police told me that Cecelia Longbourn has also been murdered. Do you think someone could be targeting the members of the knitting circle?"

"That's certainly how it looks at the moment. The police are going to provide protection for the other members."

"Good. I wouldn't want anyone else to go through this."

***

After a depressing start to the day, I needed something to raise my spirits. What better way than to take my darling dog for a walk in Candlefield park?

"Barry! I won't tell you again. Come here!"

He ignored me as per usual. I'd made the fatal mistake of forgetting his treats, so the chances of him listening to me were practically zero. He was running around and around the lake, but thankfully, so far, had not decided to go for a dip. As I got closer to the lake, I spotted a couple sitting on a bench. It was Amber, but the man with her definitely wasn't William. It was Sebastian—Aunt Lucy's new gardener. The two of them were laughing and joking. Even from this distance, I could tell they were flirting with one another. What on earth was Amber thinking?

I didn't want her to see me, so I hurried back to the top of the park and stayed there until Barry ran out of steam, and came to find me. When he eventually did, I looked back down the park; Amber and Sebastian were still together on the bench.

Back at Cuppy C, I treated myself to a cup of tea and a muffin. I was still trying to figure out what I should do about Amber, when she walked in.

"Hi, Jill!" she called—all *butter wouldn't melt*. She wasn't fooling me with her *little miss innocent* act.

"Hi." I couldn't bring myself to smile at her.

"What's up with you, misery guts?" She pulled up a seat and joined me at my table.

"Nothing."

"Come on. You look like you've lost a fiver and found a penny."

"I took Barry for a walk in the park earlier."

"Oh?" Her smile faded a little.

"I saw you there, Amber."

"I just went for a walk."

"You were with Sebastian."

"I bumped into him."

"You were flirting."

"I was *not* flirting."

"I'm not stupid. I know flirting when I see it."

"It was nothing, honestly. We were just having a laugh."

"Why were you with him in the first place? And don't give me that *bumped into him* rubbish."

"If you must know, he asked me out."

"What about William?"

"Why the inquisition? I haven't done anything wrong. Sebastian and I are just friends."

"Why were you flirting, then?"

"If you must know, Sebastian said he has feelings for me."

"Amber, grow up! He's only known you for five minutes. How can he possibly have feelings for you?"

"You're a fine one to talk. You've got half a dozen men on the go."

Wow! Below the belt.

"No, I haven't. And anyway, *I* don't have a fiancé!"

"I know." Her bravado evaporated. "I feel terrible."

"So, what are you going to do about it?"

"I don't know. You won't tell anyone will you?"

"I'm not going to lie to William for you. You have to make your mind up who you want to be with, and if you decide it's Sebastian, you have to tell William. You owe him that much."

"You're right. I know you're right, but please don't say anything to William. Not until I decide what I'm going to do."

"Okay. But make it quick. It's not fair to string him along."

"I know. I'll get it sorted I promise."

I didn't know what to do for the best. I wished I'd never seen Amber and Sebastian together. William was a great guy, and he didn't deserve to be treated that way. But then, Amber *was* my cousin, and I didn't want to drop her in it. I just hoped she'd make her mind up one way or the other quickly. I hated keeping secrets.

***

While I was in Candlefield, I decided to take a look around the market. As I was wandering aimlessly around the edge of the square, I spotted a couple sitting inside a bar which faced onto the market.

It was Pearl! And the man she was with was none other than Sebastian! What on earth was going on? The two of them were quite obviously flirting. That man was unbelievable!

I hurried past—I didn't want either of them to spot me.

Back at the flat above Cuppy C, I must have dozed off, because the next thing I knew someone was knocking on the door.

"Jill, are you all right?" Pearl let herself into the room.

"Yeah, I must have fallen asleep."

"Are you sure you're okay? We wondered where you were."

"I'm fine."

"Okay." She turned to walk away.

"Pearl, hold on a minute. I was in the marketplace earlier."

"Did you buy anything?"

"No, but I did see you with Sebastian."

She had the same guilty expression as Amber had had earlier.

"It's nothing. We were just talking. We're just friends."

"You were flirting, Pearl. I saw you."

"He says he has feelings for me."

"Really? How very surprising."

"Don't be like that, Jill. He can't help how he feels."

Apparently not.

"What about Alan?"

"I don't know what to do. You won't tell him, will you?"

"No, but you have to decide what you're going to do—stay with Alan or give him up for that playboy."

"Why would you call Sebastian that? You don't know him."

"Oh, I think I know him well enough. So who's it to be? Alan or Sebastian?"

"I don't know."

"You'd better decide, and quick. It's not fair to treat

Alan like this."

"I know. You're right. I'll get it sorted."

"You better had."

***

As soon as I got back to Washbridge, my phone rang. It was Tom Hawk.

"Yes, Tom."

"Jill, I thought you should know that we've spoken to all the other members of the knitting circle, and all but one of them have agreed to accept police protection. We're going to assign a police officer to each of them — for a few days at least."

"That's good to hear. Can't you persuade the other member?"

"We're going to need your help for that. The hold-out is your P.A, Mrs Versailles. She refuses point-blank to allow it. That's why I called. I wondered if you'd have a word, and see if you can get her to change her mind?"

I might have known.

"Of course. I'll talk to her. While I've got you on the phone — I wanted to ask whether you thought there was any sort of French connection? Considering what was written on the notes."

"There definitely isn't."

"How can you be so certain already? Surely the notes —
"

"I'm positive. Look, I shouldn't really be telling you any of this, but it's not French at all."

"I don't understand. I thought it said: *knit une, kill une.*"

"That's what it looks like, but that's not what it actually

says. It's *knit one, kill one*. According to our experts, the typewriter used to type the notes has a faulty key, so what looks like a 'U' is actually an 'O'."

"I see. So, presumably, if you can find the typewriter with that faulty key, you've found your murderer?"

"Precisely. Sorry, Jill, but I have to go. Don't forget to have a word with your P.A."

I caught up with Mrs V back at the office.

"The police have been in touch, Mrs V."

"Have they found the murderer?"

"No. It's early days yet. They told me you've refused to accept police protection."

"I don't need protecting, dear."

"Whoever is doing this appears to be targeting members of your knitting circle."

"I don't care. If anyone messes with me, they'll find themselves on the wrong end of a size seven."

"Is there anything I can do to persuade you to change your mind?"

She gave me a look which said *'not a chance'*.

"At least think about it, and let me know if you have a change of heart."

"I won't change my mind."

That woman was almost as obstinate as I was.

"Have *you* made any progress on the hunt for the murderer, Jill?"

"I've spoken to Jessie White and Arnold Crowsfoot."

"Did you learn anything of interest?"

"Not really. Is there anyone you can think of who might have a grudge against the knitting circle? Anyone at all?"

"We did have to expel a couple of members last year.

Let me see. There was Doris Drystone. She unravelled another member's knitting—a jumper. And then there was Wanda Moore. She borrowed needles from several members, and never gave them back. We simply can't tolerate that sort of behaviour."

"Do you happen to have their addresses?"

"We've got a file with all the members' names, addresses, and phone numbers in it. I'll dig them out for you."

Chapter 4

I'd finished for the day, and was on my way to the car when I spotted an advertising board showing The Bugle's headline.

Oh no! It can't be. Please tell me it isn't so.

I dropped into the nearest newsagent, and grabbed a copy. Great! Just what I'd feared.

I headed straight back to the office.

"Back again so soon?" Mrs V put down her latest knitting project—a purple and black scarf. "I thought you'd finished for the day."

"I had, but then I remembered something—err—something urgent I needed to do."

Where was that little ball of trouble? "Winky! Winky where are you?"

"Huh?" He crawled out from under the sofa, where he'd obviously been fast asleep.

"What's wrong? I was having a fantastic dream. Bella, me and Cindy—"

"I don't want to hear about your sordid dreams."

"How dare you call my love life sordid? The three of us were just about to—"

"Stop! If you tell me, I'll never be able to erase the mental image. And anyway, I have a bone to pick with you."

"A toe bone?"

Would I never be allowed to forget that?

"Look at this!" I put the newspaper on the floor, so he could see it.

"What am I meant to be looking at?"

"The headline of course!"

"'*Alien Cats*'?"

"Precisely!"

"What's it about?"

"Read it!"

"I can't be bothered! Give me the Cliff Notes."

"Apparently, there have been multiple reports of cats waving flags around."

He laughed. "Good! It looks like my students are doing what I asked them to—they're practising."

"Why didn't you tell them to practise somewhere where no one could see them? The Bugle has received numerous phone calls from worried cat owners who think that their pets have been taken over by aliens."

"Why would they think that?"

"Because cats don't normally wave flags around."

"I object to the expression: 'wave flags around'. Semaphore is a sophisticated communication system."

"I don't care what you call it. You're going to have to stop the lessons."

"Why? I'm making a small fortune."

"You've already got enough money-making scams. I'm sure you can afford to lose one of them."

"Scams? I'm hurt."

"You'll be hurting a whole lot more if you don't cancel these lessons PDQ."

"Purr Don't Quit?"

"Huh?"

"That's what you said. PDQ."

"PDQ doesn't stand for Purr Don't Quit."

"Of course it does."

"Not in the human world. It stands for Pretty Damn Quick!"

"Ah, right. That makes more sense."

"So, you'll cancel the lessons?"

"But, I get lonely in here. It's nice to have some feline company."

He was toying with my emotions; I knew he was. But I did feel sorry for him being stuck inside by himself, and I didn't want to deprive him of contact with other cats if I could help it.

"Look, if you insist on continuing with the lessons, you have to tell your students that they can't practise where anyone can see them. They must be more discreet or their owners will freak out."

"*You've* seen me doing semaphore, and *you* didn't freak out."

"Yes, but I'm a witch. I understand that cats can do these things, but most cats live with humans. If this story continues to gain ground, sooner or later someone's going to trace it back to me. Then, where will I be? I have to keep this witch thing under wraps."

"Are you saying you wouldn't want me to broadcast the fact that you're a witch?"

"That's precisely what I'm saying."

"So, for example, you wouldn't want me to make a post on FelineSocial?"

"No!"

"And you'd probably be willing to pay to keep it quiet?"

"That's blackmail."

"I'm not sure I'd call it that."

"What would you call it then?"

He thought about if for a few seconds. "Okay, you're right. It is blackmail. And make sure it's red not pink."

***

My next step was to visit the two women who had been thrown out of the knitting circle. Knitters gone rogue.

Wanda Moore lived closest to my office, so I called on her first. Her house had a name plaque on the front which read: 'Knit One'.

Hmm? Could that be a coincidence? Surely, if she was the murderer, she wouldn't have left a note which would give her away so easily. Or would she?

The woman who answered the door was quite short in stature, but had the longest arms I'd ever seen. She could easily have scratched her feet without bending over.

"Yes, can I help you?"

I couldn't stop staring at her arms.

"Sorry, I was given your name by Annabel Versailles."

She scowled. "What does *she* want?"

"Have you heard about the murders?"

Her expression softened a little. "Yes, I did. I heard it on the news when I was coming back from my sister's house. Terrible thing."

"My name is Jill Gooder; I'm a private investigator. Would you mind answering a few questions?"

"What kind of questions?"

"I understand that you were expelled from the knitting circle."

"What if I was? What does that have to do with anything?"

"Did you think you were treated unfairly?"

"Of course it was unfair. The whole thing was a farce. Those stupid women said that I hadn't returned their knitting needles. Why would I hold onto someone else's needles? It's their memories that are the problem. I gave each and every knitting needle back to its rightful owner. It's a pity they don't have anything better to worry about."

"So, it was all a misunderstanding?"

"Of course it was. Downright malicious, some of those women. And to think I used to be good friends with some of them. Rowena's husband and mine used to work together." She took a step back. "Would you like to come in? I have lots of stories I can tell you about the knitting circle."

Why not? She seemed harmless enough.

My opinion of Wanda Moore went up a couple of notches when she brought out a fresh packet of custard creams.

"Do you like these? They're all I've got, I'm afraid."

"Custard creams? They're my favourites." I took a couple, and then one more.

Wanda spent the best part of an hour carrying out a character-assassination of every member of the knitting circle, including some very juicy stories about Mrs V. As I was eating the last of my custard creams, I noticed a photo on the sideboard. It was Wanda Moore with a man who was quite a bit taller than her, but whose arms were of a more conventional length.

"Is that your husband, Mrs Moore?"

"*Late* husband. Billy was a good man and a darling husband. I never had cause to doubt him — not like some of these youngsters today. They get married one day, and divorced the next. Same with work — they can't hold down a job for more than five minutes. My Billy spent all his life in the same job, and never once complained."

"That doesn't happen very often these days. What did he do?"

"He worked in office equipment. Not the kind of stuff they have nowadays; none of those new-fangled computer thingies. I mean *real* equipment: Desks, chairs, typewriters—that sort of thing."

My ears pricked up at that. "Do you have a typewriter, Mrs Moore?"

"Me? No, dear. Never seen the need for one."

After I'd finished my tea, I thanked her for her hospitality, and went on my way. There was no doubt that Wanda Moore felt aggrieved at the way she'd been treated by the ladies of the knitting circle, but was that enough to drive her to murder? She'd denied ever owning a typewriter, but surely, if her husband had worked in office equipment all of his life, it was possible he'd brought one home at some point. Could she be lying?

***

It was the first time Kathy and I had had a chance for a proper catch-up since my 'date' with Jack. It didn't take her long to start the inquisition.

"So, what went wrong?"

"Nothing went *wrong*. It was okay, I guess."

"*Okay*? After all that build up, it was just *okay*?"

"It wasn't his fault. It's just that the suspension is like a black cloud hanging over him."

"How come he's still suspended? What's taking them so long? They must know he had nothing to do with taking that money."

"He says it's just how these things work, but it seems to me that he's not prepared to push it. And what's worse, he won't allow me to help him."

"Since when did that ever stop you?"

"What kind of start to a relationship would it be, if I ignored his wishes?"

"You're smart." She hesitated. "Or at least, that's what you're always telling me. Surely you can find a way to do something without Jack finding out."

"Yeah, maybe."

Peter arrived back with the kids just in time for dinner; they'd been swimming.

"I can swim two widths!" Mikey shouted.

"Well done you."

"I can too." Lizzie beamed.

"No you can't!" Mikey said.

"I can."

"Only with a float. Floats are for babies."

Lizzie looked as though she was about to cry.

"That's enough, Mikey." Kathy scolded him. "Remember what I said. If you aren't good between now and your birthday, then there's no drum kit."

"But Mum! It's true. Floats are —"

"That's enough."

Mikey went into sulk mode.

"Have you told Auntie Jill your news, Lizzie?" Kathy was obviously trying to take her mind off her brother's jibes.

Lizzie looked puzzled.

"Come here." Kathy whispered into her daughter's ear, and suddenly Lizzie's face lit up.

"Oh, yeah! Auntie Jill, guess what? I'm going to take part in a talent competition."

There's only one thing worse than talent competitions. No, wait. I was wrong. There's *nothing* worse than talent competitions. Still, just as long as *I* didn't have to go.

"Really? That's great, Lizzie."

"It's in a couple of days' time," Kathy said. "Don't you remember, Auntie Jill? You asked me to get you a ticket. You are still going, aren't you?"

I gave her a look. She'd never mentioned a talent competition—I would have remembered. And, she certainly hadn't asked if I wanted a ticket, but now Lizzie was looking at me with those big, hopeful eyes. What was I meant to say? *I'd rather have a root canal than sit through a talentless competition.*

"Oh, yeah. Ticket. I remember now. Of course I'm still going."

Kathy smirked. She'd trapped me again. Now I knew why she'd invited me over. She knew if she asked me in front of Lizzie that I wouldn't be able to say 'no'. That sister of mine was so conniving.

"Are you entering the talent competition too, Mikey?" I asked.

"No. It's too sissy." He was still sulking. That was something else he'd inherited from his mother. When we were kids, Kathy could sulk for days on end.

"Don't be silly, Mikey," Kathy said. "There's nothing sissy about a talent competition."

"Yes there is. It'll just be lots of girls singing and dancing and stuff. There won't be any drummers there. Drummers don't enter talent competitions."

"What will you be doing in the competition, Lizzie?" I

tried to calm things down.

"I'm going to sing."

"I didn't know you could sing."

"Mummy says I'm really good. Shall I sing for you now?"

"Not at the table, thank you." Peter looked horrified. Perhaps Lizzie's singing wasn't quite as good as she and Kathy had made it out to be.

When the kids had finished their meals, they asked to be excused. Kathy said they could go and play in their bedrooms. Once they were out of earshot, I turned to Kathy.

"Can Lizzie really sing?"

"Of course she can." Kathy beamed with pride. "She's my daughter."

"That's why I'm asking. You can't sing for toffee!"

"What do you mean? I was in the school choir."

"You were *not* in the school choir."

"Yes, I was!"

"No, you weren't. You just used to hand out the music."

"I was a substitute."

"The seventh substitute!"

"That still counts. I've got a badge and everything."

"She's got a badge," Peter said. "So it must be so."

Peter and I burst into laughter.

Kathy was not amused. "Anyway, Lizzie has a beautiful voice."

"Let's hope, for her sake, that she's inherited it from her father."

Chapter 5

The next morning, I found a parcel, wrapped in brown paper, on my desk. I was surprised Mrs V hadn't mentioned it.

"Mrs V, who delivered the parcel?"

"Which parcel is that, dear?"

"The one on my desk."

"I haven't seen a parcel. There wasn't one there when I dropped the post on your desk earlier."

"Are you sure?"

"Yes, dear, positive. I know I can get a little carried away with my knitting, but I would have noticed if someone had delivered a parcel."

"Okay." How strange.

Back in my office, I still hadn't seen my favourite feline.

"Winky? Winky, where are you?"

"What's all the shouting about?" He crawled from under the sofa. "Is there a fire?"

"Where did this parcel come from?"

"What parcel?"

"The one on my desk."

"Don't ask me. The old bag lady probably put it there."

"Mrs V says she doesn't know anything about it."

"You know what her memory's like. She's probably forgotten already."

"So, you didn't see anyone bring it in?"

"Nope. I'm going back to sleep now. Please don't disturb me again."

I wasn't sure I could take Winky's word for it that no one had been in the office. He could easily have slept right through it. And despite what Mrs V had said, it was entirely possible that she'd been so engrossed in her knitting that she hadn't seen the delivery man.

Could it be from TDO? I always had to be on my guard.

There was no label, so the parcel must have been delivered by hand. I removed the wrapping paper. Inside was a white box. Once again, there was no label or marking of any kind. I cautiously pulled open the lid. Inside was a small ornament. It was a miniature gravestone, and on it was inscribed the words: *Jill Gooder, R.I.P.*

Nice.

Which of my many admirers had sent me this lovely gift? I threw it across the room, and it hit the far wall with a satisfying thud, shattering into a thousand pieces.

Winky looked out from under the sofa. "What's a cat got to do to get any shut-eye around here?"

***

Doris Drystone lived alone in a small bungalow, close to my local supermarket. She answered the door in a dressing gown covered in pictures of mermaids. How strange! Not the fact that it was two o'clock in the afternoon. It was the mermaids' beards which had me baffled. Still, she was friendly enough, and invited me in for a cup of tea. There were no custard creams on offer, but she did a mean cupcake.

In fact, she did a 'mean' cupcake, a 'kind' cupcake, and a 'considerate' cupcake.

"Do you always name your cupcakes after human qualities?"

"No, sometimes I name them after Greek gods. I might

still have a Poseidon left from my last batch, if you'd prefer that?"

"No, these are fine. What flavour exactly is 'mean'?"

"Apricot. I've always considered apricots to be the meanest fruit."

Oh boy. The quicker I asked my questions, and got out of there, the better.

"I hope you don't mind me asking you this, Doris." I took a bite of 'mean'; it tasted much better than the name suggested. "How did you feel when you were expelled from the knitting circle?"

"It was a shock; it came completely out of the blue. I didn't deliberately unravel that jumper; it was an accident. It snagged on the zip of my boot, and as I walked around, it began to unwind. The other members tried to make out that I'd planned it, and that I was being vindictive. But it was nothing of the kind."

If what Doris had said was true, I had a certain amount of sympathy for her. I'd had a similar experience while looking after one of Mrs V's scarves just prior to a competition. Fortunately for me, I'd been able to use magic to repair the damage.

"Still, I'm over it now." Doris continued. "There are plenty more knitting circles, and besides, I've become rather partial to crocheting in the last year or so. They're a much more civilised crowd than the knitting bunch."

As we talked, I couldn't help but notice that the house was in need of a good spring clean. The curtains were grubby, and the carpets looked as though they hadn't seen a vacuum for an eon. Every surface was covered in dust. On the far side of the dining table at which we were seated, was a square patch set in the dust. Something had obviously been standing there, and it was about the right shape and size for a typewriter.

Doris must have noticed me staring at it because she said, "I really must get around to dusting one day. I do hate cleaning, don't you?"

"It's not my favourite thing." And yet, I still managed to do it more than once a decade.

"Did you used to have a typewriter there?" I gestured to the square patch.

"What use would I have for a typewriter? That's where my sewing machine used to be. It was one of the old fashioned ones that you operate with a handle. It was my mother's—she passed it on to me. It had been in the family for years. When it broke, I tried to get it repaired, but I couldn't find anyone who would do it. It's all electronic ones these days. I ended up giving it to a scrap metal merchant. There's a chap who comes around in a van about once a month; I asked him if he'd take it away."

Before I left, Doris insisted I take Poseidon with me. Despite her cupcake generosity, I found myself wondering whether she'd been telling the truth about the sewing machine. The square patch was certainly the right size and shape for a typewriter.

***

Fortunately, the section for scrap metal dealers was still in what remained of the Yellow Pages—Mrs V had long since shredded over half the directory. I worked my way through all the companies listed—the majority only collected metal when called out to do so. I was looking for a company which canvassed the same routes for scrap metal on a regular basis.

After one hour and fifteen phone calls, I finally tracked down the most likely candidate. Dance and Scrap operated a pickup truck which covered all of Washbridge—visiting each area on average once a month. It was a long shot, but worth a visit. If I could find the typewriter, which I suspected Doris Drystone had disposed of, and if that typewriter had a faulty letter 'O', then I had my man—err—woman.

"I can't give you much for that heap of scrap." A man with a ring through his nose greeted me at the gates of Dance and Scrap. "Fifty quid?"

"I'm not here to sell my car. There's nothing wrong with it."

He shrugged. "I'll give you seventy-five, but that's as high as I can go."

"No thanks." Cheek. There was at least another twenty thousand miles in that old girl. "I'd like to see Mr Scrap."

"Who?"

"Mr Scrap. Or, if he isn't in, Mr Dance."

The man laughed so hard it made his nose run. I'd never seen anyone blow bubbles through a nose ring before. It was quite disgusting.

"We don't have a Mr Scrap or a Mr Dance."

"Oh?"

"It's what we do. Scrap and dance."

"Dance?"

"Yes. I'm Charlie Watt; I run the scrap metal side of the business. My wife, Dot, runs the dance business."

"Dot Watt?"

"Yeah. She sells dance shoes, costumes, trophies—if it's dance related, she probably has it. Was it her you wanted to see?"

"No, actually, I wanted to ask about your scrap metal collections."

"Then I'm your man. Did you want to arrange a collection?"

"No. I wanted to ask about a collection you made during the last month. My grandmother had promised to give me her old manual typewriter and hand-operated sewing machine, but then she forgot and threw them out. She said someone came to the door and collected them. I thought maybe you'd still have them."

"Do you realise how much scrap we collect every week?"

"A lot?"

"Correct."

"So you won't still have them?"

"What would they be worth to you?"

"They only have sentimental value."

"I can't pay the mortgage with sentiments."

"Twenty pounds."

"Fifty."

"Do you have them?"

"Possibly. Depends if we have a deal or not?"

"I'll give you fifty pounds if they're the ones I'm looking for."

"Come with me. We separate out anything which we can sell on. We can usually get a few pounds for old typewriters and sewing machines on the flea market."

I followed him across the yard and into a small building which had rack upon rack piled high with all manner of rubbish.

"The typewriters are over there, and the sewing

machines just down there on the left. They all have a label tied to them with the date they were collected. Take a look while I go shake Percy at the porcelain."

I made a beeline for the typewriters. I checked the labels, but none of them had been collected within the last four weeks. Drat! Still, they were worth a closer look, so I examined the letter 'O' key on each of the machines — there was no sign of wear on any of them. That blew my theory clean out of the water. Charlie was still otherwise engaged with Percy, so I checked the sewing machines. One of them had been collected two weeks earlier, and it looked exactly the same size as the square patch on Doris' table.

It seemed she had been telling the truth after all.

"Did you find what you were looking for?" Charlie was back.

"No. They're not here."

"Are you sure?"

"Positive. Sorry to have wasted your time."

He shrugged. "No sweat. Can I interest you in a leotard or tap shoes while you're here?"

"No, thanks, but I'll keep you in mind if I decide to join The Coven."

"Who?"

"Washbridge's premier dance troupe. You should check them out."

***

It suddenly occurred to me that today was the day that Sebastian worked on Aunt Lucy's garden.

So, he fancied himself as something of a ladies' man,

did he? You had to admire his nerve. I mean—two-timing is one thing, but two-timing identical twins, that took some guts.

Aunt Lucy's was his last job of the day, so I hid a little way up the street, waited for him to come out, and then followed him to a coffee shop in Candlefield town centre.

I ordered a latte, and forced myself to have a blueberry muffin—just as cover, you understand. I deliberately chose a table from where I could keep an eye on him. I hadn't been there for more than ten minutes when a pretty blonde witch came through the doors. Sebastian must have been waiting for her because, as soon as he saw her, he joined her at the counter. After he'd paid for her drink, they both went back to his table.

So, this was number three!

I took out my phone and captured the two of them on video.

Cuppy C was practically empty, so when I asked Amber and Pearl to join me at the window table, they were happy to leave one of their assistants in charge.

"I have something to tell you both," I said.

"Is it something exciting?" Amber giggled.

"Do you have some juicy gossip?" Pearl said. "We love juicy gossip!"

"As it happens, yes I do."

"Ooh goody!"

"I'm going to tell you a secret even though I promised not to reveal it."

They both looked intrigued.

"Are you sure you should do that, Jill?" Amber said. "If you promised not to?"

"Under normal circumstances, I wouldn't, but I'm sure the two people who entrusted me with this particular secret will understand why I'm doing it. So, are you ready?"

"Yes, go on," Pearl urged.

"Yeah, tell us."

"The secret relates to a certain Sebastian."

"No! You promised," they said, almost in perfect unison. Then they stared at one another.

"Sebastian has been seeing both of you."

"Seeing Pearl?" Amber looked gobsmacked.

"You've been seeing Sebastian?" Pearl said. "What about William?"

"Never mind William, what about Alan?" Amber shot back.

"You can talk!"

"What about you?"

"Stop it! Both of you. You're as bad as each other. Anyway, I thought you'd like to know that you two aren't the only ones he's been seeing."

"What?" Amber was fuming.

I took out my phone and played the video. They both watched wide-eyed as the blonde witch gave Sebastian a kiss on the lips.

"I'm going to kill him," Amber said.

"Not if I get to him first!" Pearl was seething. "How dare he cheat on me."

"He was cheating on *me!*"

"He was cheating on both of you," I interrupted. "But he wasn't the only one who was cheating was he? What about your poor fiancés?"

"It's not the same thing," Pearl said.

"Totally different." Amber backed up her sister.

"It looks *exactly* the same from where I'm sitting," I said, self-righteously.

"Be quiet, Jill. We've got to plan our revenge."

I left the twins to it. If I knew Amber and Pearl, Sebastian would regret the day he decided to two-time them.

Chapter 6

As I walked along the corridor to my flat, I spotted Luther coming towards me. But was it Luther? Or was it his brother, Lou? I really couldn't tell the difference between them. They were *the* most *identical*, identical twins I had ever seen.

There was only one way to find out.

"Luther? Is that you?"

He grinned. "Who did you think it was, Jill?"

"To be honest, I wasn't sure if it was you or Lou."

"Pleeease! I don't look anything like my brother."

Was he delusional? They were absolutely identical in every way. How could he not realise it?

"I was talking to Lou last night," Luther said. "He said your date was a great success, and that he really enjoyed himself."

"He did?" Success? Not exactly how I'd have described it.

"What's wrong? Didn't you have a good time too?"

"It's a bit awkward."

"Go on, you can tell me."

"I didn't actually realise who he was."

"Who *who* was?"

"Lou."

"Sorry, you've lost me."

"I didn't know Lou was Lou."

Luther looked understandably confused.

"Who did you think he was?"

"I thought he was you."

"Me? How could you possibly confuse the two of us? We—"

"Don't look like one another. Yeah, so you said. You certainly do to me."

"How did you come to realise that Lou wasn't me?"

"The chrome."

"Chrome?"

"He has rather an unhealthy obsession with it."

"That's true." Luther laughed. "So, if Lou isn't your type, does that mean you're still on the market?"

"Not really. I'm actually seeing someone else now."

"Who's the lucky man?"

"A policeman. Nobody you'd know."

"It's funny how things work out, isn't it?"

"I thought you and Lucinda were an item."

"We were, kind of, but it just didn't work out, so I'm back on the market now." He laughed. "You don't know of any eligible young women who have a thing for accountants, do you?"

Typical! When I was single and hoping for a date with Luther, he was spoken for. Now, when it looked as though my relationship with Jack might actually be going somewhere, Luther was suddenly available.

There were times when I was convinced that someone had it in for me.

***

"Any progress with the murder enquiry, dear?" Mrs V asked, as soon as I walked into the office the next morning.

"Not a lot, to be honest. I've spoken to Doris Drystone and Wanda Moore, but I haven't made a great deal of progress. One piece of interesting information has come to light, though."

"What's that?"

"You remember the notes that were left next to the victims?"

"The ones written in French?"

"It turns out that it wasn't French after all. It didn't say *'knit une, kill une'*. It said *'knit one, kill one'*. The letter 'O' had obviously worn thin on the typewriter key, so instead of looking like an 'O', it looked like a 'U'."

"How did you work that out?"

"I can't take the credit for it. Tom Hawk, the man who's deputising for Jack Maxwell, told me. That means the whole case now hinges on finding the typewriter with the faulty letter 'O'. If we can find that, we've probably got our murderer. Do you know of anyone in your knitting circle who has an old-school, manual typewriter?"

"I don't. I used to have one myself, but that's years ago. I called her Bessie. I loved that old girl. I typed so many love letters on her."

"Focus, Mrs V, focus."

"Sorry dear, I was getting rather nostalgic there. I don't know anyone in the knitting circle who has one. In fact, the only old-fashioned, manual typewriter I've seen in the last ten or fifteen years, was at the local history museum. They have a part of the museum set up to look like a sixties office. I only know because Felicity Dale, one of the members of our knitting circle, works there. I went to see her at the museum a few months ago, and she gave me a tour. Have you ever been there, Jill?"

"Not since I was a kid." It bored me senseless.

"It's extremely interesting."

I bet. "Okay, thanks, Mrs V. I'll look into it."

I didn't want to build up her hopes, but Mrs V might just have given me the missing piece to the puzzle. Arnold Crowsfoot worked as a security guard at the local history museum, so he would have had access to the sixties office. If that typewriter had a worn letter 'O', then I might just have my man.

***

My office went suddenly chilly, and the chair at the other side of my desk began to swivel. Moments later, Colonel Briggs appeared.

"I think I'm getting the hang of this ghost thing." He looked rather pleased with himself. "I managed to attach myself to you first time."

"Well done, Colonel. Who said you can't teach an old dog new tricks? How are you settling into Ghost Town?"

"Very well, Jill, thanks. My house in Ghost Town isn't a patch on my old place, but you can't have everything. I'm just grateful to still be here, so to speak."

"Have you seen anything of Mrs Burnbridge?"

"I did pop over to her house, but I didn't attach myself to her in case I scared her. She seems to be enjoying her retirement."

"That's good to hear."

"I believe she's going to buy a bungalow on the coast. It's nice to see she's putting the money I left her to good use. Speaking of which, what's your brother-in-law done with his windfall?"

"He used most of it to set up his own landscaping business. Peter's worked for other people all his life, and for one reason or another, the jobs have never lasted. He thought it was time to be his own boss."

"What a terrific idea! He's very talented; he should do well."

"I'm sure he will, and it's all thanks to you."

"Don't mention it. It was the very least I could do."

"Peter is also going to buy a drum kit for my nephew, Mikey."

"I'm not sure that's quite such a good idea, but still, Peter knows what he's doing. Anyway, there's a reason I'm here today. I was hoping to get some advice from you."

"How can I help?"

"You know that Priscilla's taken a bit of a shine to me."

"Yes. How's that going?"

"It's so long since I dated anyone, I've lost touch. I don't know what I'm supposed to do. I wasn't sure who to turn to for advice, but then I happened to bump into your mother, and she suggested I speak to you. She said that you dated a lot of men, so you'd be in a good position to advise me."

My mother said what? We were going to have words.

"The best advice I can give you, Colonel, is the same advice I'd give to anyone: Be yourself. If you try to be something you're not, Priscilla will see straight through you."

I laughed. "See straight through you? Get it?"

He looked puzzled for a moment, but then smiled. "A joke?"

"Allegedly. Never mind. As I was saying, just be yourself."

"You're right. That's what I'll do. And when we go on our next date, should I buy her a little present?"

"It's always nice to receive a present."

"Flowers perhaps?"

"Yeah, flowers would be nice. Most women appreciate them. Or maybe chocolates. Chocolates would be perfectly acceptable."

"What about skimpy underwear?"

"No! Definitely not! Way too soon for that!"

"You're right, sorry. I don't know what I was thinking. Thank you for your help, Jill. I really do appreciate it. I'd better be going because I still find this *attaching* business a little tiring. Please give my regards to Peter, and tell him that I wish him every success in his new business."

"I can't really do that, Colonel."

"Why not?"

"How would I explain that I've been talking to a ghost?"

"Oh yes, of course. I'm a ghost, aren't I? I keep forgetting about that. Silly me. Bye then."

"Bye, Colonel. See you soon."

***

The local history museum was right next door to the library. It was a small grey building, and somewhere I hadn't visited since I was at junior school. I'd blanked that visit from my memory, but it all came back to me now. I'd been bored out of my brain, and had been amusing myself by dropping marbles off the first floor balcony. I still swear that I didn't see our history teacher below me. She came from nowhere. Still, it wasn't all bad. The visit had to be cut short after Miss Bluestairs was taken to A&E for stiches. I seem to remember Charlie Hillder was accused of causing her injury. I did the only honourable thing, and let him carry the can for it.

What? He had bad breath, so he totally deserved it.

Unsurprisingly, there was no entrance fee. Who in their right mind would pay to go in there? If they'd had any sense, they would have charged people to get out—that way they would have cleaned up.

I appeared to be the only visitor—big surprise! The reception desk was tucked away in one corner. Behind it, sat an elderly lady with a blue rinse. She greeted me with a smile.

"Hi, are you Felicity Dale?"

"Yes, I am. Do I know you?"

"I'm Jill Gooder. I'm a private investigator. I think you know my P.A, Annabel Versailles?"

"Of course, V. We're in the same knitting circle."

"So I understand. I know this is rather an unusual request, but I believe you have a section of the museum set out as a sixties office?"

"That's right, dear, we do."

"And I believe there's a manual typewriter among the exhibits?"

"Yes, there is."

"Would I be able to try out the typewriter?"

"No, I'm sorry, dear. I'm afraid I can't let you do that."

"It will only take me a couple of minutes."

"I can't allow you to touch any of the exhibits without getting permission from my supervisor."

"In that case, would you ask your supervisor if I could take a look at the typewriter? I just need to press a few keys."

"Yes, of course, but my supervisor isn't based here.

With all the recent cutbacks, he has to cover several areas."

"Could you phone him, perhaps?"

"We have to submit every request in writing."

"Could you email him, then?"

"I'm afraid we have to send it through the post."

No wonder they called this place the local history museum. It was like stepping back in time.

"Okay then. Never mind — it's not important."

"Are you sure? Because I could write him a letter, and drop it in the post tonight."

"No, really. It's okay."

I had to see that typewriter, and I didn't have time to wait for the wheels of bureaucracy to turn. I needed to distract Felicity somehow. But how? Then I noticed an unusual umbrella in the stand beside her desk. The bird pattern on it gave me an idea.

I cast the 'illusion' spell.

"How did that bird get in here?" Felicity looked in disbelief at the peacock that she saw standing where the umbrella had been. "Oh dear, oh dear. It must have come from the park. I'd better go and get security. I don't want it to make a mess all over the floor. Will you excuse me for a moment, Jill?"

"Yes, of course."

With that, Felicity scuttled off towards the back of the building. This was my chance. By casting the 'faster' spell, I was able to dash around the building in only a few seconds; I soon found the sixties office. Sure enough, there on the desk was the typewriter in question. Fortunately, there was a pile of paper next to it — to add authenticity, presumably. I fed a sheet into the typewriter, and typed the letter 'O'.

No! I couldn't believe it. The letter printed on the paper was a perfect 'O'.

I'd been so sure this was the typewriter that had been used for the notes found beside the murder victims, and that Arthur Crowsfoot had been my man. But I'd got it badly wrong.

I quickly made my way towards the exit. As I was leaving, I saw Felicity standing next to a tall man in a blue uniform.

"But it was there!" Felicity said. "Where the umbrella is now. It had blue and green feathers."

The man gave her a doubtful look. "Are you sure about this Ms Dale? Only we don't get many peacocks in the museum."

"Yes, I'm positive."

"Maybe it's gone back to the park."

I felt a little guilty at making her look silly, particularly as it had all been to no avail.

Chapter 7

I was back to square one with the knitting circle case. If the murderer wasn't Arthur Crowsfoot, then who was it?

Suddenly, Mrs V came rushing into my office. She looked panic-stricken.

"Mrs V? Are you okay? Don't tell me another one of your knitting circle has been murdered?"

"No, thank goodness."

"What is it then?"

"I'm so sorry. With all the upset, I completely forgot to tell you."

"Tell me what?"

"I should have remembered."

"It's okay. But what exactly did you forget to tell me?"

"There was a telephone message for you. Late last night, after you left. They said that a tax inspector would be coming to see you this morning."

Oh bum!

"She's here now. I'm really sorry."

"Don't give it another thought, Mrs V. You've had much more important things on your mind."

I hated all things tax—especially paying them. But why would a tax inspector want to see me now? I was up-to-date with my filings as far as I was aware. Maybe, if I climbed out of the window, walked along the ledge, and then climbed through one of the windows into Armitage, Armitage, Armitage and Poole, I might be able to avoid her. Or I could just make myself invisible?

But what would that achieve? Those people never gave up; she'd keep coming back until she caught me. I might as well get it over and done with.

"You'd better show her in, please."

I took a deep breath and hoped for the best. And then, in walked my neighbour, Betty Longbottom. I'd totally forgotten she was a tax inspector. Suddenly, things didn't seem quite so bad. Betty and I were friends, and I'd helped her out of a tight spot with the police, so she wouldn't do anything to hurt me or my business. What a stroke of luck!

"Hi, Betty."

"Miss Longbottom, if you don't mind."

"Sorry?"

"I'm here in my official capacity as a tax inspector, so I'd be grateful if you would address me as Miss Longbottom."

"Are you kidding?" She didn't answer, but I could tell by her expression that she wasn't. "Okay, *Miss Longbottom*. Would you care to take a seat?"

"Thank you." She sniffed the air. "Is it my imagination? Or is there a very strong smell of cat in here?"

"He's over there." I pointed to Winky who was resting after his latest semaphore class. "He doesn't smell." Much.

"Hmm?" She screwed up her nose.

Mrs V came back into my office; she was carrying a small pile of scarves.

"I forgot to ask you, young lady. Would you care for a scarf? I have all colours and sizes. I have socks too, if you'd prefer those?"

"I'm not allowed to accept gifts of any kind. It's against the rules. Tax inspection is a very sensitive area. It's essential that we're seen to be squeaky clean."

I almost choked. Betty Longbottom — *squeaky clean*? This was the woman who'd been shoplifting as a hobby for years; the woman who had an Aladdin's cave of stolen goods in her apartment, and who'd asked me to rescue her from the police when she'd been caught red-handed. It was only because I'd used magic to hide the contraband that she'd got away with it. Now, she had the audacity to sit there, and say that she couldn't accept a scarf because it might be seen as a bribe! The two-faced little madam!

Mrs V backed out of the room.

"So what is it that you want, Bet—err, Miss Longbottom?"

"We've had reports, Miss Gooder."

"What kind of reports?"

"Reports that you're paying your staff *off the books*."

"How do you mean, *'off the books'*? And anyway, I don't have any staff."

"What about the woman out there; the woman with the scarves?"

"That's Mrs V. She's not really staff. She's—well, I suppose *in theory* she's my P.A."

"What's that if it's not staff?"

"Basically, Mrs V just knits all day."

"But she does answer the phone?"

"Occasionally. If she's not knitting anything too complicated."

"And she does greet people when they arrive?"

"I suppose so. She usually offers them a scarf or a pair of socks."

"How much do you pay her?"

"Nothing."

"Come, Miss Gooder. Do you really expect me to believe that? Who in their right mind would work for you for nothing?"

"I don't ask her to work for nothing."

"So you *do* pay her?"

"No."

"Do you pay her under the table?"

"I don't pay her *under* the table, *on top* of the table or *behind* the table. I don't pay her at all. She chooses to come here because she'd rather do that than stay home alone."

Betty gave me a sceptical look. This could turn nasty. No one was ever going to believe that Mrs V came to work without pay. It was far more likely that they'd think I was paying her 'cash-in-hand' so as to avoid tax.

I had to kill this investigation quickly, and the best way to do that was to remind Betty that she owed me a favour.

"By the way, Miss Longbottom, did you have a clear-out yet?"

"Sorry?"

"Those items in your spare bedroom; the ones that the police were interested in?"

"I'm not here to discuss my personal affairs, Miss Gooder. I'm here to discuss whether or not you are defrauding the tax office."

"Oh, okay. I just assumed you'd prefer no one found out about that."

"You're not threatening me, are you, Miss Gooder?"

"Of course not. Because that would be a very serious offence. No threats involved here."

"I think the only way to resolve this matter is for me to speak with your accountant."

Hold on just a doggone minute. Betty knew full well that Luther was my accountant. She must have heard he was no longer in a relationship. All this was just a clever ploy, so that I'd arrange for her to meet with him. The crafty little madam!

"You want to meet with Luther?"

"Is *he* your accountant?" She feigned surprise. "I hadn't realised."

Yeah right! This woman could lie for England.

"I'm sure you hadn't. I'll have a word with him, and ask him to contact you. What's your office phone number?"

"It would probably be easier to get him to call at my flat."

I bet.

"But surely, you want to keep this official, Miss Longbottom?"

"I'm not investigating Luther—err—I mean Mr Stone, so it will be okay."

"I just bet it will."

"Sorry?"

"I said, I'll be happy to ask him to get in touch with you."

"Good." She stood up. "Hopefully, he'll be able to resolve this issue to my satisfaction."

"I'm sure Luther will do his best to satisfy you."

At least she had the good grace to blush as she left.

What a conniving little minx!

After Betty had gone, Mrs V came into my office.

"I'm sorry about that, Jill. I forgot all about it."

"It doesn't matter."

"Is there a problem?"

"Hopefully not. She actually lives in the same block of flats as me."

"Who? The tax inspector woman?"

"Yes, we're meant to be friends."

"She didn't act very friendly."

"I know. I've helped her out on a number of occasions, and yet all she's ever done in return is attack me with sea creatures, and now go after my taxes."

"Sea creatures?"

"It's a long story. I won't bore you with it."

***

I'd had a phone call from Pearl. She'd asked me to meet her and Amber straight away outside Bar Electra in Candlefield town centre. What were those two up to this time? Nothing good, I'd wager.

I magicked myself over there.

"What's going on?"

"Shush!" Amber put a finger to her lips. "Look who's in there."

Seated at the bar was Sebastian who for once was alone.

"We have a cunning plan." Amber grinned.

Oh dear.

"You two wait here," Pearl said. "I'm going in."

Amber and I stayed outside and watched. Sebastian greeted Pearl with a smile and a peck on the cheek, as she sat on the stool next to him.

"What's going on Amber?" I whispered.

"I called him earlier, and told him that I'd meet him here. He thinks Pearl is me."

"Let me get this straight. He thinks that's you in there?"

"Yeah."

"Okay, so what happens next?"

"Just watch."

It was Amber's turn to walk into the bar. As she did, I

cast the 'listen' spell, so I could hear what was being said. She walked straight up to Sebastian and Pearl.

"Sebastian! How could you!" I had no idea Amber was such an accomplished actor. "What are you doing with Pearl?"

He looked at the twin who was sitting next to him. "Pearl? But, I thought you were Amber."

"Why did you arrange to meet Amber?" Pearl said. "I thought you and I were an item?"

"Wait a minute!" Amber interrupted. "I thought you and I were seeing one another?"

"I—err—you—err—I." He glanced back and forth between the two of them. The twins had him totally flustered.

While he was still in a state of confusion, Amber picked up his drink, and poured it over his head. Pearl did likewise with her drink. When the two of them came out of the bar, they were both red in the face from laughing.

"That'll teach him to cheat on us." Pearl sounded indignant.

"Yes. It's terrible what he did," Amber said.

How very self-righteous the two of them were. And how very two-faced! Apparently, the fact that both of them had been cheating on their fiancés didn't count.

***

Back in Washbridge, I'd just climbed into my car when my phone rang. It was Mrs V.

"Jill, have you heard?"

"Heard what?"

"They've arrested Wanda Moore for the murders."

"Are you sure?"

"It was on the news just now."

"Right. I'll try to get hold of Tom Hawk to find out exactly what's happened."

I made the call, and remarkably got through to him first time.

"Jill, you and I can't keep flirting like this. Jack will think I'm taking advantage while he's away."

I wasn't in the mood for his humour — if that's what it was.

"Tom, I understand there's been an arrest in the knitting circle murders."

"There has. It's not a secret. It's been on the news."

"Wanda Moore?"

"That's right. Look, what I'm about to tell you has to be completely off the record. Okay?"

"Yes, of course."

"We found a typewriter in her basement, and the letter 'O' matches the 'O' on the notes that were found next to the victims. It looks like this particular case is closed. There's nothing more for you to do."

"Have you charged her yet?"

"No, but it's likely that we will very soon."

"Okay, thanks. Look, while I've got you on the phone, is there any word on what's happening with Jack?"

"It's still with Internal Affairs, as far as I know."

"It's taking forever."

"These things always do."

"Isn't there anything you can do to help?"

"Me?" He laughed. "Internal Affairs work to their own timetable. Nothing I or anyone else says or does will change that."

"Okay. Thanks anyway."

Who were these Internal Affairs people, and why did they work at a sloth-like pace?

Once I was back home, I went over the knitting circle murders in my mind again. I'd had my own suspicions about Wanda Moore as soon as she told me that her late husband used to work in the office equipment business. And, I'd thought it was strange that she'd never had a typewriter. Surely, it was the sort of thing her late husband might have brought home from time to time. It turns out that she'd been lying all along. Perhaps I should have pursued it further. Maybe, I should have found a way to search her house. But it didn't matter now. The police had come through on this one without my help. Now they had the typewriter with the faulty key, they had their murderer.

Case closed.

Chapter 8

Winky's ears pricked up as though he'd heard something, and then he hissed. A few moments later, I heard something too. It took a few moments for me to realise what it was—the sound of someone giggling. Were the twins playing some kind of prank on me? Were they hiding somewhere? There was nowhere in the office for them to hide unless they'd made themselves invisible.

"Pearl? Amber? I know you're here. Stop messing around."

But it was the colonel who appeared. On his arm was Priscilla—the source of the giggling.

I cleared my throat. It was the only way I could get their attention; they were so busy gazing into one another's eyes.

"Whoops." The colonel said. "Sorry, Jill."

"Yes, sorry." Priscilla giggled again.

"I take it you two are now an item?"

"Very much so." The colonel beamed. "All thanks to you and Darlene. We thought we should pop in to tell you how grateful we are."

"Yes, thanks ever so much, Jill." Priscilla gushed. "I would never have dared to approach Briggsy myself."

Briggsy? Oh, dear.

"It's a pity you don't have a young man, Jill." The colonel said. "Isn't there anyone special?"

"Despite what my mother may have told you, I am actually seeing someone."

At least, I thought I was.

"That's great news. Anyone I know?"

"A detective. He worked on the Vicars case, and on—" I

bit my tongue just in time.

"My murder?" He smiled. "It's okay, you're allowed to say it."

"Sorry that was a little insensitive."

"Was it love at first sight?" Priscilla interjected. "Like me and Briggsy?"

"Not exactly. It was more hate at first sight. But things have improved a lot since then."

"There's something else I need to speak to you about, Jill." The colonel's tone was much more serious now. He turned to Priscilla. "Would you mind, Cilla?"

"Not at all, Briggsy." She giggled again, and then disappeared.

"Cilla and Briggsy?" I laughed. "Really, Colonel?"

"I know. If the men who served under me ever find out, I'll be in for a lot of ribbing."

"I think it's sweet."

"Anyway, as I was saying, there's something important I need to tell you, and I'd rather Cilla didn't hear this."

"Is something wrong?"

"I fear it might be. Earlier today, I happened to overhear something in Ghost Town. Something rather disconcerting."

"About what?"

"About you."

"Me? Why would anyone be talking about me in Ghost Town?"

"It's related to the murder of Edna Vicars. Do you remember that thug who was put away for his part in the jewel heist?"

"How could I forget him? What did he call himself? Battery?"

"Yes, that's him. Apparently, another prisoner took a dislike to him, and stabbed him. He's dead."

"I had no idea."

"Murdered in his cell. And he blames you."

"Blames? As in, present tense?"

"He's now a resident of Ghost Town. A friend of mine overheard him mention your name. It seems he blames you for getting him locked up in the first place, and he's hell-bent on revenge. I thought I'd better let you know."

"Right, thanks for the heads up, Colonel."

At least now I knew where the gravestone ornament had come from.

"If I hear anything else, I'll let you know, Jill."

"Okay, thanks very much."

As if things weren't bad enough. I already had TDO after my blood — now I was being targeted by a ghost too.

***

After what the colonel had just told me, I thought I'd better have a word with Mad. Rather than ask her to come to the office, I decided to pop into the library.

There was no sign of her behind the reception desk. The woman who was sitting there, looked at me over her glasses as though I was something the cat had dragged in. According to her badge she was the *'Senior Librarian'*.

"Excuse me," I said.

"Yes, how can I help?"

"I'm looking for Madeline."

She rolled her eyes. "Madeline? She could be *anywhere*. That girl is a liability. I've no idea why she was given this job. *I* had no say in it."

"So, you don't know where she is?"

"No. As I said, she could be anywhere."

"But she is in today, is she?"

"Oh yes, she's in. I saw her first thing this morning, but I haven't seen anything of her since then. I suppose it's too much to expect her to do any work."

I had a sneaking suspicion that this woman was not Mad's biggest fan.

I walked up and down the aisles of bookshelves looking for Mad, but there was no sign of her. I was just about to give up when I heard a noise that seemed to come from behind a door at the far end of the library. Then I heard something fall onto the floor; it sounded like a tin can.

The door wasn't locked so I sneaked inside. It was obviously some kind of store room. And there was Mad. She was holding what appeared to be a small crossbow. In front of her, lined up on a shelf, were a number of empty drinks cans.

"Mad?"

She jumped. "Jill, you scared me to death. I didn't hear you come in."

"Sorry. What on earth are you up to?"

"I was bored, so I thought I'd have a bit of target practice."

"Surely you don't use that thing against rogue ghosts?"

"This toy? No, of course not, but it helps to keep my eye in. I use a G-gun when I'm ghost hunting, but I can hardly use that in here."

"Don't you get in trouble for hiding away, and using a crossbow?"

"Not so far. To be honest, I think Anita is just glad to get me out of the way. I'm a bit of a liability out there."

"Anita?"

"The Senior Librarian."

"Right. I just met her."

"Laugh a minute, isn't she?"

"She seems to take herself rather seriously."

"Tell me about it."

"By the way, what happened with Troy?"

Troy was Mad's ex. He'd come in search of her, and I'd managed to stall him while Mad made her getaway.

"He caught up with me at my mum's place."

"Is he still trying to persuade you to go back to London with him?"

"No. I scared him off."

"How did you manage that?"

"It was remarkably easy, as it happens. I told him that I was a librarian. That was enough to put him off me for life. He said he preferred sexy Mad rather than boring librarian Madeline. To be honest, I do too, but I didn't tell him that. Anyway what brings you here?"

"I've got a bit of a ghost-related problem, and I hoped you might be able to help."

"I will, if I can. What's up?"

"There's this guy — well ghost, really. He goes by the nickname of Battery."

"Battery? Seriously?"

"Afraid so. His real name is Joseph Truman. He was arrested as a result of a murder investigation I was working on. He wasn't implicated in the murder, but he was sent down for an unrelated incident. It seems that while he was in prison, he was murdered by another prisoner. Anyway, I've just had a visit from the ghost of an old friend, Colonel Briggs. He was murdered recently too."

"People seem to drop like flies around you."

"I know. The colonel popped in to see me because he'd heard rumours that Battery is out for revenge. He wants me dead, apparently. And the other day, I found a parcel on my desk, which contained a small ornament—a gravestone with my name on it."

"Charming. And you think this Battery guy left it there?"

"Mrs V is adamant that no one came into the office to deliver it. And Winky confirmed that he hadn't seen anyone either. So, yeah. I think it must have been Battery's ghost."

"Okay. I'll make some enquiries in Ghost Town to see what I can find out, and I'll get back to you."

"Thanks, Mad. Can I have a go with the crossbow?"

**

"Do I have to go?" I groaned.

"Yes you do." Kathy was as uncompromising as ever.

"How long will it last?"

"I don't know, Jill. Three hours, probably."

It was the night of the talent competition. I'd only promised to go because Lizzie was taking part. I hadn't realised that it was open to all ages. The prospect of watching three hours of talent-less people was enough to make me weep.

"Where is Lizzie anyway?" I said, as we made our way to the community hall.

"Pete took her earlier. The contestants have to be there

an hour before the competition starts."

"If she's one of the first on, can we leave after we've seen her?"

"No, we can't. We're going to stay until the very end."

"That could be days away."

"Is there anything you don't complain about, Jill?"

"Custard creams."

The community hall was absolutely heaving with people. They must all have been friends and relatives of the contestants. Either that or they'd been taken there at gun point.

What? Why else would any sane person be there?

The first two acts were beyond bad. So far beyond that it wasn't even funny. When the third act came on stage, I recognised the three women immediately. Not so very long ago, they had appeared in my office, wearing the same sparkly leotards, and had tried to recruit me.

"Please welcome your next act on stage. Ladies and gentlemen, give it up for The Coven," the compere said.

The three women broke into a dance routine. It was different from the one they'd performed for me, and to be honest, it was much better. They'd obviously spent a lot of time on their choreography, but I couldn't help but wonder if they actually had any time left for seeking out and destroying TDO.

At the end of their routine, they all got down on one knee, then jumped up one by one, and shouted, "We. Are. The Coven."

I turned to Kathy. "I could have been the 'The'."

"What?"

"This dance troupe came to my office, and tried to

recruit me."

"Don't be ridiculous." She laughed for some unknown reason. "Why would anyone ask you to join their dance troupe?"

"It's true."

"You can't dance."

"Obviously *they* think I can. That's why they wanted me to be the 'The.'"

"What do you mean: be the 'The'?"

"Did you see the finale just now? Where one of the women got up and said, 'We', the next one got up and said, 'Are', and the last one got up and said, 'The Coven.'"

"Yes, I thought it was very effective."

"They felt it would be even better if instead of having one person say 'The Coven', they would let me say 'The', and someone else say 'Coven'. I was to be the 'The'."

Kathy shook her head. "Sometimes I worry about you, Jill."

Thirty minutes later, Lizzie came on stage. I'd never actually heard my niece sing before—trust me, I would have remembered. On a scale of nought to ten, she was beyond awful. Imagine a cat being attacked by a violin, and you have some idea of how bad she was. I had to do something to help, so I cast a spell, which affected everyone in the hall. Instead of hearing Lizzie's screeching, they heard a beautiful voice. The whole audience was captivated. When Lizzie had finished, everyone stood up and applauded. Lizzie looked absolutely thrilled as she ran off the stage.

At the end of the evening, the awards were announced.

Lizzie didn't place in the overall competition, but she came first in the 'eight years and under' section—much to her and Kathy's delight.

"Well done, Lizzie."

"Thanks, Auntie Jill."

"Yes, well done, you." Kathy hugged her daughter.

"I'd like to enter some more competitions, Mummy."

"That's a great idea." Kathy beamed. "We'll keep an eye open for other competitions in Washbridge or maybe even a bit further afield. I think you could have a future in music. What do you think, Auntie Jill?"

I just smiled. What was I meant to say? I could hardly tell them that in the next competition Lizzie entered, she'd probably be booed off the stage, unless I happened to be around to use magic on the audience again.

As Kathy and Lizzie were collecting their coats, I bumped into The Coven girls who had come a very creditable third in the overall competition.

"Hello again, you three."

"Oh hi, Jill," Brenda said. "Did you catch our act?"

"I did. It was very good. You've obviously been working on your routines."

"Thanks. We've put in a lot of work, haven't we, girls?"

The other two nodded.

"How's the hunt for TDO going?" I asked.

"To be honest, we've decided to focus on the dance. We're going to leave the search for TDO to those more qualified than us."

"That's probably a wise decision."

"We'd still love it if you joined us though. You'd make an excellent 'The.' Is there any chance you might change your mind?"

"I'm flattered, Brenda, but I'm going to have to pass on that one."

Chapter 9

There was a lot of activity in the outer office when I arrived at work the next day.

"Morning, Mrs V."

"Morning, Jill. I hope you don't mind, but we're having a breakfast meeting of the knitting circle. We haven't seen one another since the tragic incident with Cecelia and Rowena, so we thought we'd try and boost morale by getting together."

The other ladies all forced a smile, but there was a definite sense of melancholy in the room.

"We're all still in shock," Mrs V said. "Not just because of the loss of two dear friends, but also at the realisation that Wanda Moore could have done such a thing."

"She obviously held a grudge after being expelled from the group."

"But it was such a silly, trivial reason to take two people's lives."

As we were talking, I spotted Felicity Dale seated at the back. I felt I owed her an apology, so as I made my way to my office, I tapped her on the shoulder, and whispered, "Felicity, could you spare me a minute, please?"

"There's a cat asleep on your desk, Jill."

"That's Winky. He lives here."

"How sweet. They don't allow us to have pets at the local history museum. If they did, I'd take my dog, Barney with me. Would you like to see a photo of him?"

"Sure." I just can't get enough of dog photos.

"There he is." She produced a tattered photo from her purse—no smartphones for Felicity.

"He's very handsome." For a flea-bitten old mongrel. "Look, Felicity, I just wanted to apologise for storming in on you like that the other day."

"Don't worry about it." She waved my apology away. "I'm sorry that I was so distracted. It was that peacock. You saw it, didn't you?"

"Yes, of course."

"I'm so relieved to hear you say that. By the time I'd fetched security, it had disappeared. He probably thought I'd imagined the whole thing. I still can't understand how it got into the building."

"It's a mystery." I really should be on the stage. "But then, they're strange creatures, peacocks."

"I wrote to my supervisor to ask him if you could try out the typewriter, but I'm afraid I haven't heard back yet."

"Don't worry about it. It doesn't matter now."

"It's probably just as well because there was a problem with it. If I remember correctly, the letter 'O' had partially worn away. It looked almost like a 'U'."

What? Not when I tried it, it didn't. Not that I could tell Felicity that.

"Are you sure? I thought those old manual typewriters were indestructible."

"I'm positive. We tested it when we were setting up the office. I typed 'The lazy black fox jumped over the quick cat'. Or was it 'the slow brown fox jumped over the quick dog'? Something like that. The letter 'O' looked just like a 'U'."

"Is it possible you hit the 'U' key by mistake?"

"No. I tried the letter 'O' several times, and each time it came out like a 'U'."

Felicity went back to join her colleagues in the outer office, and left me wondering what on earth was going on. I'd been absolutely sure that the typewriter in the museum had been the one used to type the notes left with the victims, but when I'd tested it, the letter 'O' had been fine. And yet, according to Felicity, the letter 'O' *had* been worn. How could that possibly be?

And then the penny dropped.

***

Daze was all by herself in Cuppy C; she looked down in the dumps. To be fair, she was never a smiley, cheery, laugh-a-minute kind of girl, but today, she looked particularly fed up. She was at a table next to the window—staring down into her coffee cup. She hadn't even noticed me come in.

"Hi, Daze."

"Oh, hi, Jill. I didn't see you there."

"Do you mind if I join you?"

"Sure. Pull up a chair."

"I'll just get a coffee first. Do you want anything?"

"No. I'm okay, thanks."

She definitely sounded out of sorts, so I asked the twins if they had any idea what was wrong.

"She's been like that since she came in," Pearl said.

"Yeah, she's been very quiet." Amber glanced across at Daze. "We didn't like to say anything though. That would be asking for trouble."

"I'll see if I can get to the bottom of it." I glanced at the display of cakes. "Where are all the blueberry muffins?"

"We're all out, sorry. We've got double chocolate, though."

"Go on then. I'll make do with one of those." The hardships I had to endure!

Back at the table, I decided to bite the bullet, and try to find out what was wrong.

"Are you sure you're okay, Daze? You seem a bit down in the dumps. Is Blaze okay?"

"Yeah, he's fine. He still insists on wearing those stupid luminous catsuits. He thinks I don't know, but I have my spies."

"Is that why you're so down?"

"No, of course not. That doesn't bother me. That's just Blaze being Blaze."

"What is it then?"

"It's something and nothing really. When I signed up to be a Rogue Retriever, I joined at the same time as four or five others. We went through training together, and have become close friends as well as work colleagues. Now, suddenly, out of the blue, three of them have decided to quit."

"All at the same time?"

"Yeah. They're going to start a small business together—a petting zoo."

"That's quite the career change."

"I know. I was amazed when they told me. They asked if I wanted to go in with them."

"Don't you fancy it?"

"It's not really my thing. I'm not that big on animals. Plus, I'm allergic to rodent fur. It would be no good me working there. I'd be sneezing all day long."

"I can see how that would be a problem."

Note to self: don't introduce Daze to Hamlet.

"I guess that exodus is going to leave you short in the

Rogue Retriever department?"

"You're not kidding. I had enough on my plate before all of this happened. Now, my bosses have shoved all the orphaned cases onto me. I don't know how I'm ever going to get through them all."

"Are they recruiting new Rogue Retrievers to replace them?"

"Yeah, but it's going to take time."

"I imagine it will. It's not everyone who could do your job."

Suddenly, her face lit up for the first time since I'd arrived. "I've just had a brilliant idea."

"What's that?"

"The powers-that-be said that if I recommended anyone for the post of Rogue Retriever, it was pretty much guaranteed they'd get the job. They trust my judgment, apparently."

"That's quite a compliment. Do you have anyone in mind?"

"I hadn't really given it much thought until now, but there is one obvious candidate."

"Who's that?"

"You, of course."

"Me?" I laughed. "That's a joke, right?"

"I never joke about work." It was true. Daze wasn't exactly known for her stand-up.

"You can't be serious. I could never do your job."

"Why not?"

"Because I'm only a level three witch. You're a sup sup. I could never do what you do."

"Do you actually know what a sup sup is?"

"Well, I—err—thought it was like—err. No, not really."

"The clue is in the name. It's a sup who has powers beyond other sups of their kind. "Doesn't that pretty much describe you?"

"What do you mean?"

"I can't think of another witch who has moved from level one to level three as quickly as you did."

"Yeah, but that doesn't mean anything."

"And, didn't you score highly in the Levels competition?"

"I guess."

"And haven't you regularly cast spells which are considered way above your level?"

"Well, yeah, but—"

"So, all in all, I would say that makes you a very special level three witch. A sup sup, perhaps?"

"I'm nothing like you."

"Not yet, maybe. But, with a little time and the right training—"

"I don't think so."

"The money's really good. It's not something I generally discuss, but we are paid a ridiculous amount of money for what we do. And from what the twins tell me, your P.I. business isn't doing all that well."

Why were the twins talking about my business behind my back?

"The business is just going through a bit of a dry spell at the moment. It's nothing to worry about."

"In that case, surely the extra money would help? It's not like you'd have to give up your business in the human world. It's something you could do alongside it. You'd make a pretty penny."

"I really don't think it's for me. I already have a second

job in Cuppy C."

"But, from what the twins tell me, you're not really cut out to work behind the counter."

Great! Thanks girls! I needed to have words with those two.

"I might make the odd mistake." Or ten. "But, I'm still learning the ropes."

"Wouldn't you rather do something a little more exciting, and better suited to your skillset?"

"I'm not sure I'd be any good at it."

"You'd be great. I'd have no qualms about putting your name forward."

"No, Daze. I'm sorry. You're going to have to look elsewhere."

"Look. Why don't you at least spend some time with me? See what the job actually entails, and then decide. If you don't like what you see, you've lost nothing. But if it turns out that you think you'd enjoy the job, then I'll put your name forward."

"I'm going to have to think about it."

"Okay, but don't leave it too long."

"I won't. I'll let you know in a couple of days."

***

It was nine-twenty-five in the evening when I arrived at the park. It was dark, and there was no one else around. The solitary lamppost gave out just enough light to see a few yards in each direction. In another five minutes, I'd know if my hunch about the knitting circle murderer was correct or not.

I heard footsteps coming towards me, and a figure

appeared out of the shadows.

"Hello, Arnold. I've been expecting you."

Although elderly, he still cut quite an intimidating figure.

"I take it you received my letter?" I said.

His face was contorted with anger. "You shouldn't have interfered." He pulled out a knitting needle, and started towards me. I stood my ground.

"Why did you do it Arnold? Why did you kill your wife?"

"The ungrateful cow got what she deserved. After everything I'd done for her, she said she was leaving me. She called *me* selfish. *She* was the selfish one. After all the sacrifices I've made. I warned her I'd never let her leave, but she wouldn't listen."

"So you killed her?"

"It was her own fault."

"And what about your friend Cecelia? Was it *her* own fault too that you murdered her?"

"I didn't want to kill Cecilia, but what choice did I have?"

"Plenty actually. But then, I guess you thought that killing Cecelia would cover your tracks. It would make it look like someone was targeting the knitters circle."

"That stupid knitters circle. Rowena cared more about those women than she did about me."

He lurched forward, but I cast the 'faster' spell, and stepped to the side so quickly that he flew past me. As he did, I tripped him, and sent him falling to the ground. Then, before he could get up again, I cast a spell to bind his hands and feet.

At ten o' clock, as arranged, Tom Hawk arrived with

two policemen who took Arnold away. Tom stayed back to speak to me.

"You really shouldn't have done this alone, Jill. It could have been dangerous. Why did you tell me to come at ten when you knew he'd be here at nine-thirty?"

"If you'd been here earlier, Arnold might have spotted you, and been spooked. Anyway, I was never in any real danger. It will take more than an old man with a knitting needle to see me off."

"How did you know it was him?"

"I suspected him from the beginning. I was convinced he'd typed the notes on the typewriter in the local history museum where he worked. I was right. But he was much cleverer than I gave him credit for. After he'd typed them, he exchanged the letter 'O' key for the same key in Wanda Moore's typewriter while she was away at her sister's house. The ironic thing is that Wanda Moore had no idea there was a typewriter in her basement. But Arnold knew because he and Wanda's husband had worked together in the office supplies business before Arnold retired and took up his new role in security."

"Clever and very devious." Hawk nodded. "But I still don't know how you managed to flush him out, and get him to meet you here."

"I contacted an office supplies company — one that still deals in the old manual typewriters."

"I'm surprised any of them still do."

"It took a while, but I eventually located a small family business which provides spares and maintenance to the few hold-outs who refuse to upgrade their beloved manual typewriters. I got them to file down the letter 'O' on one of the machines which they keep for spares. Then I typed a letter to our friend Arnold." I reached into my pocket and pulled out a sheet of paper. "This is a copy of it."

Tom Hawk studied it for a few seconds.

"It's gobbledegook."

"Not if you change some of the 'U's to an 'O'.

Meet me at Washbridge Park, by the streetlight near the bridge, at nine-thirty. Bring five thuusand puunds ur I gu tu the pulice."

"Ah, I see. So he knew someone was onto him?"

"Yes, and he had no intention of paying them off because he feared that whoever it was might keep coming back for more money. He brought his knitting needle instead."

Chapter 10

"Good morning, Mrs V."

She didn't look up, but instead continued to stare at her knitting.

"Mrs V? Good morning."

She obviously hadn't heard me, so I waved my hand in front of her face. When I finally got her attention, she removed her ear plugs. No wonder she hadn't been able to hear me.

"Why are you wearing those?"

"Because of all the noise coming from your office."

I listened for a few moments. "I can't hear anything."

"It keeps stopping and starting."

"What kind of noise?"

"Music of some kind."

If Winky had got his DJ console out again, I would swing for him.

"I'll see to it."

Winky was lying on the sofa with his paws clamped over his ears; there was no sign of the DJ console. But now I could see where the music was coming from. Next to the far wall, was a piano, which appeared to be playing itself.

What the?

A man's ghostly figure appeared on the seat in front of the piano.

"Alberto?"

"Hi, Jill." He stopped playing and turned to face me.

I loved that man's Welsh accent. But, I digress.

"You're probably wondering what I'm doing here."

"Kind of. Yeah."

"Your mother's to blame. She nagged me to get a hobby,

but then when I did, she complained that she couldn't hear the TV when I was playing."

"I'm still not sure why you're in my office."

"Darlene banned me from playing in the house, so I needed somewhere else to practise. It was your mum who came up with the idea of coming here."

"Did she now? That was good of her."

"I told her that it might not be convenient, but she said you rarely had any work on."

Thanks Mum!

"You can stay for a while, but then you and your ghost piano will have to go somewhere else, I'm afraid."

"Ghost piano?"

"Isn't that what it is?"

"No." He laughed. "There's no such thing as a ghost piano. It's a real one."

"Of course. Silly me."

"If it's okay with you, I'll just play for another hour or so, and then I'll get out of your way. Darlene will just have to put up with it."

"Sure, that's fine."

He began to play again—it wasn't really my kind of music, but there was no denying he had a certain talent. I stood behind him to watch more closely.

"Jill?" I hadn't heard Kathy walk in behind me.

Oh bum!

How was I meant to explain this? I had to think on my feet, and quick.

I whispered to Alberto, "Keep playing."

I started to move my hands across the keys—hopefully from where Kathy was standing it would look as though it was me playing.

"How long have you been able to play the piano?"

"Some time now. I took lessons last year."

I still had my back to her, and was trying to follow Alberto's hand movements with my own.

"You never mentioned it. Aren't you meant to sit down when you play?"

"I find I play better when I stand."

"Well, I have to say, you're very good. You should teach Lizzie and Mikey."

I whispered to Alberto. "On three, stop playing. One, two, three."

He stopped, and I turned around to face Kathy.

"I'm not really qualified."

"But you're so good. And, they could use your piano."

"I have to get rid of it. The landlord said it's against my tenancy agreement."

"Pity. But hey, I've just had a great idea. You could enter the next talent competition with Lizzie."

"Yeah. I don't think so."

Fortunately, it was only a flying visit, and Kathy couldn't stay for long.

"Sorry about that, Jill," Alberto said, after she'd left. "I rather dropped you in it."

"That's okay, but the piano has to go."

"I understand, and I'm sorry. It will be gone within the hour. I just need to organise transport."

"No problem, but do me a favour. Please tell Mum I'd like a word with her, would you?"

***

Shortly after Alberto had taken his piano away, Mad popped into the office.

"I've done some checking, Jill. You're right about that thug, Battery. He's definitely plotting to get revenge on you. Unfortunately, I can't do anything about it unless I catch him in the act. You should be safe for now because he only recently entered the ghost world, and it takes a while for new ghosts to get their full range of powers. He's quite capable of visiting the human world for just a few seconds, as he did to deliver that parcel, but there's no way he would have enough strength to kill you at the moment. The problem is, once he does, he could strike at any time."

"What do you suggest I do? I can't just wait around until he decides to bump me off."

"If I were you, I would try to draw him out now while he's still relatively weak."

"I thought you said he wouldn't be able to come into the human world for more than a few seconds. That doesn't give me time to do much of anything."

"He'll be strongest at the place where he lived just before his death."

"That was prison."

"Before that. Where did he live before he got sent down? Do you know?"

"Yes. With his girlfriend, Hilary Vicars."

"Then you need to somehow get into her house and draw him out. If you can do that, and if I can catch him in the act of attacking you, then I can have him sent back to Ghost Town, and you'll be safe."

"That sounds dangerous, but I suppose it's better than simply hanging around, waiting for him to get the jump on me. I'll see what I can arrange, and keep you posted. Thanks for your help, Mad."

***

I was sorting my rubber bands by size and colour when my phone rang. It was Kathy.

"Hey, Jill. Are you busy?"

"Quite busy, yeah."

"That's a pity."

"Why? What's up?"

"I'm bored to tears. I wondered if you fancied coming down to Ever for a chat."

"You're usually run off your feet. How come you're bored?"

"Come down here and you'll see for yourself."

"Like I said, I'm pretty snowed under, but I suppose I could spare half an hour. I'll be there in a minute or two."

The rubber bands would just have to wait.

"I'm just popping down to Ever, Mrs V. Do you need anything while I'm there?"

"No thank you, dear. I'm stocked up on yarn at the moment."

"I shouldn't be long."

When I got there, the place was almost empty. There was one person in the shop itself, and only another two in the tea room. I'd never seen it so empty; it was usually a struggle to get through the door.

"What's going on, Kathy?"

"Look over there." She pointed across the road to the new shop, Best Wool, which was now open. It was crammed full of customers.

"What does Grandma have to say about that?"

"She hasn't been in yet today, thank goodness. She'll

blow a fuse when she sees the shop is empty. And I dread to think what she'll have to say about that crowd across the road."

"Why don't I go over there for a few minutes to see what I can find out about the competition?"

"Go for it." Kathy nodded.

The sales assistant on the door of Best Wool was handing out goody bags, which contained Wonder Needles.

"What are these exactly?" I acted dumb. What do you mean, that shouldn't have been difficult?

The sales assistant gave me the spiel.

As I'd suspected, they worked just like Grandma's One-Size Knitting Needles. Oh dear, this wasn't looking good.

Best Wool was packed. There were free drinks and cakes on offer, so to stay under the radar, I helped myself to a couple of cupcakes. As I munched away on the first one, an assistant approached me, and asked if I'd be interested in Never-ending Wool.

"What is that exactly?"

"The way it works is that you pay a subscription, and then the wool lasts forever. The price of the subscription depends on how many different colours you want to use. It's the cheapest wool subscription available in Washbridge."

"I see. Okay, well I'll have to think about it, thanks."

So, not only were they selling their equivalent to One-Size Knitting Needles, but they were also running their own wool subscription service in direct competition with Everlasting Wool. And, they were offering both at a cheaper price. Grandma really was in big trouble. She'd invested a lot of money in Ever A Wool Moment; this new competitor could put her out of business.

Suddenly, I heard a familiar voice. It came from a man standing in the middle of a predominantly female crowd. It was Miles Best, and standing at his side was his girlfriend and business partner, Mindy Lowe. Now it all made sense. The owners, M and M, were none other than Miles and Mindy.

When Grandma found out, all hell would break loose.

Back at Ever, I told Kathy what I'd seen. Obviously I couldn't tell her I knew the owners — that would have led to some awkward questions.

"I'd better get back to the office."

"Why don't you come over tonight. I'll let you know how your grandmother takes it when she finds the shop half empty."

"I can already guess her reaction. She's going to be on the warpath."

"Come over anyway. Unless you're seeing Jacky boy."

"I haven't heard from him, and I don't like to phone. I'm not sure he'll be in the mood for a night out until this suspension thing gets sorted out."

"So you'll come over?"

"Why not?"

Back in the office, I stared at the pile of rubber bands. Is this what it had come to? I had zero paying clients at the moment, and the rent would be due soon. I had to do something, so I made a call.

"Jill?" Daze sounded surprised to hear my voice.

"I've been thinking about what you said."

"About becoming a Rogue Retriever? That's great. I'll put your name forward."

"Hold on. Don't let's get ahead of ourselves. You said I could spend a day with you first to see what I thought of it."

"Yes, of course. I'll sort something out and get back to you."

Oh boy! What had I just let myself in for?

***

I'd rung the bell twice, and knocked as loud as I could, but no one had answered the door. I knew Kathy and Peter were in because I could hear the TV.

"Kathy? Peter?" I used my key to let myself in.

"We're in the lounge," Kathy shouted.

"Didn't you hear me at the door?"

"Shush! Have you seen this?" She pointed to the TV. "Someone's been murdered in Coffee Triangle."

'Earlier this evening, a man, who has yet to be identified, was shot and killed in Coffee Triangle. No one appears to have seen or heard the shooting even though the shop was crowded with customers at the time.'

The reporter then turned to a young man at his side.

'I believe that you were in Coffee Triangle at the time of the murder?'

'That's right. I was playing a drum, when someone screamed, but no one seemed to know why. Then someone else screamed, and then slowly everyone stopped drumming, and someone shouted, "He's dead!" The next thing I knew we were being ushered out of the shop. Then the police arrived.'

'Did you actually see the victim?'

'No, I was sitting at the other side of the shop, but I heard someone say that a young woman had asked him to move up,

and when she touched him on the shoulder, he fell face first onto the table.'

'But you didn't hear a shot?'

'No, but there was so much noise in there with all the drumming that it's unlikely anyone would have heard it.'

'Right, thank you very much. And now, back to the studio.'

"You should investigate that." Kathy muted the TV.

"I'm not the police. I don't just go around investigating random crimes. I take on cases for paying customers."

"I thought it would keep your hand in."

"I don't think so. But it doesn't look good for Coffee Triangle. I don't imagine many people will be queuing up to get in there after this."

Chapter 11

The next morning, Jasper James was behind the counter at the newsagent. As always, he was wearing his trademark fedora — today's was green.

"Good morning, Jill! What can I do for you this beautiful morning?"

"I'm after a copy of The Bugle. I want to see what they have to say about the shooting in Coffee Triangle. Did you hear about it?"

"I did indeed. Terrible affair. Quite a few people have bought The Bugle this morning for that very reason. Would you like to make it a regular order? I can have it delivered to your flat if you like."

"No, thanks. I'm not a big fan of this paper."

"What about a magazine. I know just the thing for you."

"I doubt it."

"How about Witch Magazine?"

Wow! This man was good.

"You must have heard of it. It's the leading consumer magazine — they review all kinds of stuff: broadband, mobile phones, pogo sticks. You name it, they cover it."

"Ah, you mean 'Which'?"

"That's right. Would you like me to sign you up for a subscription?"

"No, I'm okay, thanks."

The Bugle didn't disappoint. It had the usual ridiculous headline: *'Bang the Drum'*. There wasn't a great deal of substance to the article, but they had managed to interview the woman who'd been sitting opposite the victim. According to her, the man had fallen face first onto the table. It seems that everyone thought he was drunk, but then someone noticed the blood, and realised that he'd been shot. No one heard the gunshot or saw a gun. Tom Hawk, the detective in charge of the case, had appealed for anyone with information to come forward.

***

In a moment of madness, I'd agreed to spend the day with Daze. I still couldn't see myself as a Rogue Retriever, but the P.I. business was slow, and according to Daze, Rogue Retrievers were well paid, and it was steady work. I owed it to myself to at least give it a shot.

We'd arranged to meet in the market square in Candlefield, by a cake shop called 'Temptation'. It was aptly named because the window was full of delicious looking muffins and cupcakes. I hoped Daze would hurry up because I didn't think I could resist them for much longer.

"Jill! Sorry I'm late." Daze appeared behind me.

"Hi, Daze. Oh? Hi, Blaze. I hadn't realised you'd be joining us today. So, what's the plan?" I said, with one eye still on the cake shop.

"Not eating blueberry muffins, for a start." Daze had seen me staring at them.

"Sorry, yeah. What will we be doing, then?"

"First off, we need to call at a shop a couple of streets from here. Follow me."

The sign above the shop read 'Cat's Suits'.

"Shouldn't that be catsuits?" I said.

"No." Daze laughed. "The owner's name is Catherine.

Everyone calls her Cat, and she sells suits—hence: Cat's Suits. But she also has a range of catsuits as well."

What a weird world I lived in.

Cat was a fine figure of a woman, and could easily have been a Rogue Retriever herself. She greeted Daze and Blaze like long lost friends.

"Hey, Blaze. Are you still interested in those luminous catsuits you asked me about?"

Daze shot Blaze a disapproving look.

"Luminous catsuits?" Blaze shook his head, and did his best to look as though he had no idea what Cat was talking about.

"You asked me about them last week."

"Me? No, that wasn't me. You must be confusing me with someone else."

Cat looked puzzled. She obviously wasn't aware that Daze didn't appreciate Blaze's taste in the more outlandish catsuits.

"Cat, can I introduce you to Jill Gooder?" Daze said. "She splits her time between here and Washbridge where she's a private investigator."

"That must be interesting work."

"Yes. It can be."

"Jill is spending a day with us to see if she'd like to become a Rogue Retriever."

"That's something of an honour, Jill," Cat said. "I expect you'll find it very exciting. A bit dangerous though, but I suppose in your line of business you're used to that."

"Yes, I'm quite excited." Terrified more like.

"Well, first things first," Daze said. "You need to pick out a catsuit."

"For me?"

"Of course! You can't possibly enjoy the full Rogue Retriever experience unless you're dressed properly."

Cat led me towards the back of the shop where there was a vast selection of catsuits in every colour known to man.

"I quite like the green one. The dark green one that is — not the luminous one, obviously."

Daze gave me a nod of approval.

I went through to the changing room, slipped out of my clothes and into the catsuit. It was a tight fit, and pinched a little, but it looked okay.

"What do you think?" I stepped out of the changing room.

Daze gave me a thumbs up.

"Green is definitely your colour," Blaze said.

To complete the outfit, Daze gave me a mesh net which was similar to the one that I'd seen her use numerous times to capture rogue sups.

"Give it a try!" she said.

"Really? On what?"

"On Blaze."

"Hold on a minute!" he objected.

I quite liked the idea, so I threw it over him and sure enough he disappeared.

"Don't worry about him." Daze laughed. "He'll be back in a minute or two."

**

I was just beginning to think how good I looked in the green catsuit when Daze told me that I had to get changed.

"Why what's wrong with this?"

"Nothing, but we have to go undercover. We're on the trail of a rogue wizard. Blaze and I have been after him for ages. I've just had a tip off that he's due to do his weekly shop in the Seven Days supermarket in Washbridge."

"What do you want me to do?"

"You and Blaze will be stacking shelves. I'll be working on the checkout."

"Typical," Blaze said under his breath.

"Pardon?" Daze glared at him.

"Nothing. I didn't say anything."

We magicked ourselves over to Washbridge, and as we made our way to the supermarket, Blaze whispered to me, "She always gives herself the best jobs."

"Don't let her hear you."

"Maybe I should have taken that job with Taze." He sighed.

"My ears are burning." Daze looked over her shoulder. "Is he moaning about getting all the bad jobs again?"

"No. He was just saying what a good boss you are."

"Now, I know you're lying."

The manager at the supermarket seemed to be expecting us. Somehow, with practically no notice, Daze had managed to get us onto the payroll.

Daze was on the checkout nearest to the door, so she could watch people coming and going. Blaze and I were given trolleys, full of goods that we had to put on the shelves. I'd never realised just how hard stacking shelves could be. I'd always thought it looked like a cushy job. Trust me, it wasn't.

By late afternoon, I was exhausted. My back and legs were aching, and I desperately needed to sit down. But then, suddenly, Daze came flying around the corner, in pursuit of a man. It was obviously the rogue wizard, and he was headed my way. I waited until he was just a few feet away, then pulled out the net, and threw it over him. He disappeared in a puff of smoke.

"Well done, Jill," Daze said. "Great catch."

"Thanks. What do we do now?"

"You'd better come back to Candlefield with me. You can help to process him, so you get to see exactly what's involved."

Back in Candlefield, the wizard was behind bars and looking none too happy.

"I haven't done anything wrong," he protested. "I don't know why you've brought me here."

"Save it for someone who cares." Daze waved his complaints away. As promised, she showed me how to complete the paperwork, which was then passed to the officer on duty.

"So?" Daze said when the three of us were back in Washbridge. "How did you enjoy your day?"

"It was very tiring, and a little boring for the most part, but it livened up when we caught the wizard."

"That's how it tends to be. It can be quiet for hours, but then it's all go. So what do you think? Can I sign you up as a Rogue Retriever?"

I shook my head. "I'm sorry, Daze. It's really not for me."

"I thought you'd jump at the chance. Is it the catsuit you don't like? You could always have a different colour."

"No. I love the outfit. In fact, if it's all the same to you I'd like to hang onto it."

"Of course. But what about the money? It pays well, and I know you're struggling with the rent."

"You're right, but there's just too much standing around, doing nothing. I'd be bored out of my skull."

"Okay. But if you change your mind."

"I'll give you a call."

***

After I'd left Daze and Blaze, I called in at the office to check if there had been any messages, and to feed Winky who I found playing with a yo-yo. I hadn't seen one of those since I was about ten years old.

"What are you doing?"

"Splitting the atom. What does it look like?"

Remind me again. Why did I put up with this cat?

"Yo-yos are for small children, aren't they? They're so boring. Up and down, up and down—yawn!"

"Not when you're a grand master, like me. Watch! This is called 'the sleeper'." He threw the yo-yo towards the ground. At its lowest point, it seemed to stall, as though it was sleeping, and then it shot back up. "Did you see how I made it sleep?"

"Huh. Anyone can do that." The last time I'd played with a yo-yo, I could barely get it to go up and down, but I wasn't about to tell him that.

"Okay, what about this one, then? This one's called 'the forward pass'."

This time he threw the yo-yo out in front of him, and back it came. Then, out in front of him again, and back it came again.

"Pah!" I mocked. "Nothing special about that."

"Okay, well what about this? This is called 'around the world'."

He threw the yo-yo out in front of him, but then sent it in a huge arc before catching it again.

"Hmm? Not bad, I suppose."

I was actually really impressed, but there was no way I was going to tell him that.

"Not bad? That was brilliant. Watch this one."

He threw the yo-yo to the side, and when it came back, he caught the string on his other paw, and let the yo-yo swing left and right, left and right, and then it shot back up and he caught it.

"Okay. I admit that was good. What do you call that trick?"

"That's 'the trapeze'."

"So anyway, why the sudden interest in yo-yos?"

"I became a yo-yo grand master years ago, but I'm a little rusty. I need to get back up to speed before the competition."

"Which competition?"

"The Feline Yo-Yo Masters' competition."

"When's that?"

"Soon. I'll need you to provide transport for me, obviously."

"I might be busy."

"I'll give you a share of the prize money."

"How much is it?"

"Two thousand pounds for first place."

"Two thousand pounds?"

"Yep."

"And, do you have a good chance of winning?"

"The money's as good as mine already."

"Okay, we'll split it fifty-fifty."

"Eighty-twenty," he countered.

"Sixty-forty."

"I'll give you thirty percent, and that's my final offer."

"Okay. Done."

Chapter 12

I thought I'd better check how things were going at Ever, and if the new competition had affected takings.

The shop was still very quiet, but the tea room was absolutely buzzing. When I managed to catch up with Kathy, she looked even more harassed than usual.

"It's crazy in here, Jill. Absolutely crazy!"

"How come? What's going on?"

"It's because Coffee Triangle is closed. A lot of the people who would normally go in there have come in here instead because we're just up the road. Look at those people over there. They're drumming the tables with knitting needles because they're missing their fix of drums. Takings are through the roof."

"Grandma must be pleased."

"Not that you'd notice. She's still seething about the competition across the road."

"My ears are burning." Grandma appeared at our side.

"Good morning, Grandma, I didn't see you there."

"Are you interrupting my staff again?"

"I was just having a few words with my sister, if that's okay?"

"Just make sure you're quick about it. We're really busy in the tea room today."

"So I see. Terrible business at Coffee Triangle."

"Not so terrible for us. We're going to have a record day."

"That's a bit heartless, Grandma; a man was killed."

"Yeah, well, business is business. Just don't spend too long chatting. There are customers to attend to." With that, she disappeared.

"That woman is all heart." I shook my head in disbelief.

"What did you expect?"

A horrible thought crossed my mind. Grandma was completely ruthless when it came to business, but surely even she would draw the line at murder just to close down a competitor. Wouldn't she?

If not, Miles and Mindy had better watch out.

***

I knew I had to heed Mad's warning. Battery might not have the strength to attack me just yet, but if I ignored the threat, he soon would have. I'd rather confront him on my terms, at a time and place of my choosing, rather than have him creep up on me out of the blue. I intended to end this right now, and to do that I'd have to confront him in the house which had once belonged to his ex-girlfriend, Hilary Vicars.

The next door neighbour was out in the garden. At first, I thought she was weeding, but then I realised she was actually having a conversation with the garden gnomes.

Oh boy!

"I don't care if you're cold, Harold, you can't come in the house. Look at Angela; she isn't complaining, is she? Oh dear, John, have those horrible cats been peeing on you again?"

"Hello?" I tried to catch her eye.

She straightened, and began to rub her back.

"Hello, dear. I didn't see you there. I was busy seeing to my little ones."

"Right."

"They're such hard work. Do you have any?"

"Gnomes?"

"Shush! Don't call them that. They don't like it."

"Sorry. No, I don't have any."

"Take my advice. Don't start. You buy one. Then another. And, before you know it, you're overrun with them. They take over your life."

"I'll remember that." I'd have to make this quick before someone realised this woman had escaped. "Does Hilary Vicars still live next door?"

"No, dear. Hilary moved out some time ago. The cat lady lives there now."

"Cat lady?"

"She's got thousands of them. Noisy, smelly things. They're always peeing on the little ones—especially John. Between you and me, he's beginning to smell."

"I'm sorry to hear that. You don't happen to know if she's in, do you?"

"Who?"

"The cat—the woman next door?"

"She's in most of the time, dear. Never goes anywhere. Just to the shops to buy cat food occasionally."

After I'd thanked her, she returned to the conversation with her little ones. Note to self: Never buy a garden gnome.

When I knocked on her neighbour's door, a thousand cats began to meow. After a few moments, an old woman answered the door; her grey hair looked as though it hadn't seen a brush since Woodstock.

"What do you want?" Her breath smelled of tuna. "I saw you talking to the gnome lady. Has she been complaining about me again?"

"No. I—"

"She's crazy that one. Talks to them, you know—calls them her little ones. I keep my doors locked—you never know, do you?"

"I'm actually from the cat sanctuary."

Her scowl changed to a smile. "Oh, right. How can I help you?"

"I'm collecting old clothes and bric a brac. Anything really that we can sell at the jumble sale. All proceeds go to the cat sanctuary. I wondered if there was anything you could let us have?"

"I'm sure there is, dear. I'm always happy to help the local cat charities. Do come in. I'll see what I can sort out for you."

There were cats everywhere, and I had to tread carefully to avoid stepping on any of them. The place smelled strongly of cat, but to be fair they all seemed to be well cared for.

"Why don't you go through to the lounge, dear. I'll go upstairs, and sort out some stuff for you."

"Okay. Thanks very much."

The last time I'd been in that room, I'd interviewed Hilary Vicars and her ugly boyfriend, Battery. But now, it was full of cats, and they were all eyeing me suspiciously. A few of them rubbed around my legs; others had their backs arched, and were hissing.

"Come on, Battery," I said, out loud. "I know you're here. Come out and face me."

Nothing.

"Come on. Show that ugly face of yours if you dare."

Suddenly, the temperature in the room dropped, and all

of the cats began to hiss.

"Come on, Battery. You're not afraid of a woman, are you?"

And there he was; larger than death, and even uglier than I remembered.

"I'm going to finish you!" he yelled.

"You always did talk a good game."

"It's your fault I'm dead. Why didn't you just keep your nose out. No one cared about Hills' mother."

"The colonel did. And, I'm pretty sure Hilary did too."

He moved closer, and reached for my neck. Was it possible for a ghost to strangle me? If Mad didn't hurry up, I'd soon find out. Battery's hands were almost on my neck when, right on cue, Mad burst through the door. She lassoed him first time, and he disappeared in a puff of smoke.

I breathed a sigh of relief. "Thanks, Mad. I owe you one."

"No problem. You won't have to worry about him again, Jill. All his haunting privileges will be revoked. I'd better get back to Ghost Town to book him in. See you around."

"Bye, Mads, and thanks again."

The cats were still hissing and spitting when the old lady came back downstairs, carrying a pile of clothes.

"What's the matter with this lot?" She glanced around. "They seem to have taken against you."

"Cats never did like me."

"Strange that you would choose to work at the cat sanctuary, then."

She tried to pass me the clothes.

"I've just had a phone call while you were upstairs. It

seems there's a bit of a feline emergency. There's a cat stuck down a drain—I need to go and rescue him. Can I call around tomorrow to pick these up?"

"Yes, of course. We can't leave the poor fellow down a drain, can we?"

***

The outer office was crowded. It was Mrs V's weekly knitting class, which she held at lunchtime for the staff of Armitage, Armitage, Armitage and Poole. I wasn't sure if it was my imagination, but there seemed to be more and more people attending every week. She really should have charged for the lessons. She would probably have made more money from knitting lessons than I could ever afford to pay her.

There were so many chairs squeezed into such a small space that it was a struggle to make my way through to my office.

"Hello, Jill," a few of the knitters greeted me. I'd come to know some of the regulars.

"Hi, everyone. How's it going?"

A few of them held up their latest knitting project. Mrs V was some kind of hero in their eyes, and rightly so.

As I passed by Mrs V's desk, she held up her hand to catch my attention. "Jill, can I have a quiet word in your office, please?"

"Sure. Come on through."

We managed to pick our way through the throng of knitters. Once inside my office, she pushed the door closed behind her. All very cloak and dagger.

"This might sound strange," she said, in little more than

a whisper. "But I think Gordon Armitage is spying on us."

The thought that he would spy on us wasn't all that strange; he'd bugged my office before. Armitage had wanted me out ever since he'd moved in next door, but that was never going to happen despite his numerous attempts to get me evicted.

"How do you mean?"

"I think he's infiltrated the knitting class."

"I don't follow. How do you mean *infiltrated*?"

"I think he's out there right now — dressed as a woman. It's obviously him. He's not fooling anyone."

"Are you sure?"

"Yes. He's over by the door. You can check for yourself."

"Okay. We'll go back out there. But act casual. Let's not draw attention to ourselves."

I followed Mrs V into the outer office, picked up a file, and pretended to read it. I was actually looking over the top of the file, towards where Mrs V had said the infiltrator was sitting. I spotted him straight away. It was quite obviously Gordon Armitage. He was wearing a ridiculous wig, and his dress was a terrible fit. Did he really think he could fool a private investigator of my calibre with that poor excuse for a disguise?

This simply wasn't on. He'd caused me enough problems already. I wasn't about to let him sit in my office, and spy on me, so I walked across the room and stood directly in front of him.

"How did you ever think this would fool anyone, Gordon?"

He looked up — clearly surprised. He obviously hadn't expected me to rumble him so easily.

"Did you really think you could pass yourself off as a woman with that ugly mug of yours?"

Then he did something that took me totally by surprise. He burst into tears. He was surely taking this a bit too far?

"You can forget the act, Gordon. The game is up. I know it's you. Why don't you take your sorry backside back to your office where it belongs?"

He was crying inconsolably now, and I almost felt sorry for him, but I still wanted him out of there. I was about to tap him on the shoulder, and tell him to be on his way when the outer office door burst open. I turned around to see Gordon Armitage standing there. I glanced back and forth between the two Gordon Armitages — one standing in the doorway, and the other crying inconsolably in the seat in front of me.

It was the Gordon Armitage standing next to the door who spoke first.

"What's going on in here? Rebecca! What are you doing here? No sister of mine is going to spend time in this office."

The crying Gordon Armitage looked up. His eyes - or should I say, *her* eyes - were blotchy and red. Rebecca? It was Gordon's sister.

"Don't worry, Gordon," she said, through her tears. "I'll never come back here again. I've never been so insulted in all my life."

"I'm very sorry," I said. "I thought—"

"Get out of my way." She pushed me aside. "Wait for me, Gordon. I won't stay in this place another second. I should have listened to you. You were right. She *is* a horrible woman!"

With that, the two of them left.

Everyone stared at me as though I was some kind of monster. And, who could blame them?

Oh bum!

Chapter 13

I felt awful about what I'd said to Gordon Armitage's sister. I had to get out of the office—away from all the other knitters who no doubt now thought I was a horrible person.

As I walked down the street, I noticed there was a police car parked outside Ever.

Inside the shop was Tom Hawk; he was with two uniformed police officers. The three of them were standing at the counter; Tom was arguing with Grandma.

"I'm not going anywhere!" Grandma said.

"If we could just have a few words in the back, there would be no need for you to go to the station." Tom Hawk spoke in a cool, calm, collected way.

"I've got nothing to say to you." Grandma was giving him the evil eye.

This was not going well, so I thought I'd better step in to try to calm things down.

"Tom, is there a problem?"

"Hi, Jill. I'm sorry about this. We'd like a few words with this *lady*, but she isn't being very cooperative."

"This is my grandmother, Tom. What is it you want to talk to her about?"

"Don't talk about me as though I'm not here." Grandma wasn't about to stay silent for anyone.

"Oh, trust me, I know you're here, madam," Tom said. "I'm in absolutely no doubt about that. Look, this is just a routine enquiry. We're talking to all the coffee shop and tea room owners in the area about the recent incident at Coffee Triangle."

"But why? What could that possibly have to do with my

grandmother?"

"Again, I'm still here!" Grandma's wart was beginning to glow red—never a good sign.

"Grandma, why don't you just go into the back with Mr Hawk, and answer his questions. That will be an end to it."

I could sense that what she really wanted to do was to turn him and the other two officers into something hideous. But, even *she* wouldn't be able to get away with something as blatant as that in Washbridge.

"Very well." She sighed. "Come on, young man. Let's get this over with."

"Shall I come with you?" I offered.

"No, you stay there." Grandma fixed me with her gaze. "I don't need you to hold my hand."

It seemed like forever, but it can't have been more than fifteen minutes later that Tom re-emerged; he looked decidedly the worse for wear.

"Is everything okay?" I asked.

"Your grandmother is a real piece of work."

"No arguments from me there. Did you get what you needed?"

"Not exactly. She told me I was wasting my time, and that she had nothing to say to me."

"Why are you talking to her anyway? What possible good can it do?"

"Like I said before. It's just routine. We have to consider motive, and the fact is that there are too many coffee shops and tea rooms in this area. One or two of them have been struggling recently. They're bound to benefit from Coffee Triangle's closure, if only temporarily."

"You can't seriously be suggesting that the motive for that man's murder was to close down Coffee Triangle?"

"I'm not suggesting anything, but there's no denying that this shop, along with others, has obviously benefited from the closure. See for yourself." He pointed to the tea room which was packed with customers.

"Look, Tom, Grandma may be a little difficult."

"That's the understatement of the year."

"But she wouldn't resort to murder just to get a few more customers through the door."

"I'm sure you're right, Jill. Anyway, we have several more shops to visit. Hopefully, your grandmother will calm down soon because I may need to speak to her again."

After the police had left, I thought I should check if Grandma was okay.

She wasn't. She was fuming.

"How dare he come in here and question me? How dare he throw around such accusations?"

"I'm sure he didn't actually accuse you of anything."

"Of course he did! He more or less accused me of murder."

"Do you think you might be overreacting? Just a little?"

"Overreacting?" Her face turned a shade of red I'd never seen before.

"Sorry, but I'm sure it'll all be cleared up soon."

"I doubt that. I could tell by the way he was talking that he's already decided I'm guilty. He won't rest until he's thrown me in jail."

"I'm sure that isn't going to happen."

"You're dead right it's not. Because you're going to sort this out for me."

"Me? What can I do?"

"You're a private investigator, aren't you?"

"Err, yeah."

"Right. Well, the sooner you find out who *did* murder that poor man, the sooner you get the police off my back. It is now your top priority to discover the identity of the murderer."

"Hold on! I'm not a police officer; I'm a private investigator. I only investigate things if someone's paying."

"Then I will pay you!"

"Huh?" I was well and truly gobsmacked. Had I heard right? Had Grandma just offered to pay me? "You mean you want to hire me?"

"Yes! Unless of course you've got too much work on already. I need someone who can give it their full attention."

"Err—well, I am rather busy," I lied. "But, you *are* family, so of course you will get top priority."

"I assume I'll also get a family discount."

"I suppose I could give you five percent."

"Thirty percent? That's very kind of you. I expect this to be resolved within the next few days. Understood?"

"Understood."

Much to my relief, the knitting class had disbanded by the time I got back to the office.

"I'm sorry about the upset just now, Mrs V."

"It was as much my fault as yours, dear. I was positive it was Armitage."

"Not much we can do about it now. Anyway, on a brighter note, I have a new case."

"That's nice, dear. What is it this time?"

"I've been hired by my grandmother."

"Oh dear. That sounds like bad news. She'll probably expect you to work for nothing."

"Amazingly, she's actually promised to pay me; less a family discount, obviously."

"And what exactly is it she's hired you to do?"

"She wants me to find out who murdered the man in Coffee Triangle."

"Why would she care?"

"When I was in Ever just now, the police were there. They're talking to all the local coffee shop and tea room owners who have benefited from Coffee Triangle's closure. Grandma did not take kindly to what she considered to be an interrogation. She feels that the police are looking to pin the murder on her, so she wants someone to find the real murderer, and clear her name."

"And she thought of *you*?"

"You don't have to sound quite so surprised. I am a private investigator, and I am her granddaughter. Surely I'm the logical choice."

"Of course you are. It's just that I didn't think you'd want to work for your grandmother. I can't imagine she's going to be the easiest client you've ever had."

"I'm sure you're right. But any case is better than no case at all, and at least she's going to pay me. So, I guess I'd better make a start."

I'd done P.I. work for Aunt Lucy in the past, and I hadn't charged her. But Grandma was different. With all the money she was making, why shouldn't I bill her? In fact, I might just stretch out the case, and add in a few expenses here and there. Yeah, I could make quite a killing with this case.

Okay, okay. It was a poor pun under the circumstances. Sheesh!

***

"There's a young woman to see you," Mrs V had her knitting with her when she walked into my office. "Sorry about this dear, I'm at a critical point. I didn't want to put it down."

"Name?"

"I haven't given it a name yet. Perhaps green glow scarf?"

"I meant the name of the young woman who wants to see me."

"Oh yes. Silly me. Dorothy Babs, I think she said."

"I think you'll find it's Dorothy. Babs is her dog. Send her through, would you?"

I'd first met Dorothy in the park when Barry and her dog, Babs, had become friends. She'd mentioned she wanted to move to the human world, and I'd managed to get her an interview for a job in Washbridge. I'd also given her a contact for a flat share.

I could tell by the look on her face that things were going well.

"Sorry to turn up out of the blue like this, Jill. I just wanted to come by and thank you for your help. I'm not sure I could have made the move without you. I landed that job in the fancy dress shop that you put me on to."

"You did? That's great."

"Yeah, I've only been there a while, but I'm slowly

learning the ropes. It's a strange set-up because the humans who come into the shop have no idea that the people running it are actually sups. It's weird to hear them say things like: *'That's not something a vampire would wear'*, when it quite obviously is. They all want glitzy, cutesy costumes which no self-respecting vampire would be seen dead in. Still, it's lots of fun, and the people I work with are fantastic."

"Did you move into the apartment as well?"

"Yeah, I did. It all worked out great. They're a nice bunch. We get on really well, and the apartment's lovely. It's much better than I thought I'd be able to afford, but sharing with two others just about makes it doable."

"How are you finding life in the human world?"

"I'm enjoying it. I wasn't sure what to expect, but most of the humans I've come across are really friendly. It's not that much different to living in Candlefield."

"That's what I thought you'd find."

"Except for one thing." She picked nervously at a fingernail.

"What's that?"

"That's the other reason I came to see you today. I hope you don't mind, but I don't really have anyone else to talk to."

"No problem."

"I'm not sure what I expect you to do. It's silly really."

"Go on, spit it out."

"You're probably already aware that in Candlefield vampires drink synthetic blood. There are factories which produce it, so there's a ready supply."

"Yes, my cousin's fiancé, Alan, mentioned it. Is that the problem? Can't you get it here in Washbridge?"

"No, that's not it. It's easy enough to get synthetic blood here. There are several outlets which cater for vampires living in the human world."

"So what *is* the problem, then?"

"As you know, there aren't any humans in Candlefield, so there's no temptation to drink human blood. In fact, between you and me, I've never drunk it. But, here in Washbridge, there are lots of humans, obviously. So the temptation is much greater."

"But if you've never drunk it —"

"I know. It never occurred to me for one moment that there would be a problem. I thought I might not get on with humans, or that I might miss Candlefield. It never entered my head that I'd feel the urge to drink human blood."

"But you do?"

"Yes, something rotten. Every time a human comes into the shop, or even when I'm just walking down the street, I can almost taste their blood. I just want to bury my fangs into their neck, and drink. It's terrible."

"I hope you haven't acted on that impulse."

"No, of course not. I would never do that. At least, I hope I wouldn't, but the urge is so strong. The vampire who used to work in the shop before me was found drinking human blood, and taken back to Candlefield by a Rogue Retriever."

"I know. I was the one who reported her."

"You're not going to report me, are you?" She looked terrified.

"Of course not. You haven't done anything wrong, have you?"

"No. I'm just scared that I might. I don't know what to

do. If only there was somebody I could talk to—somebody who could help."

"Look, why don't I ask around. I know a few vampires. I'll see what I can find out, and hopefully I'll come up with something."

"Would you, Jill? I'd be so grateful."

"Are you sure that you're going to be able to resist in the meantime?"

"I won't do anything stupid, I promise. I carry a small bottle of synthetic blood in my bag at all times. If I do feel the urge, I just have a quick drink from that, and it seems to get me through—for now at least."

"Leave it with me, Dorothy. I'll see what I can do, and I'll get back to you. How's Babs, by the way?"

"She's fine. I'm sure she's missing me, but she's staying with my mother, Dolly. She'll be spoiling her to bits. She gives her way too many treats. What about Barry? Is he okay?"

"Yeah, he's as daft as ever."

"Okay. Well, I'd better get back to the shop. I'm on my lunch break."

Poor Dorothy. It must have been horrible to be surrounded by tasty meals, and not be able to take a bite. I had the same problem with blueberry muffins.

Chapter 14

The next morning, the police tape had been removed from outside Coffee triangle. There was still a 'Closed' sign on the door, but I tried it anyway. To my surprise, it wasn't locked.

"Hello! Is anyone here?"

"We're closed," said a voice from the back. "We'll be open in a few days' time."

"Actually, I just wanted a word with someone."

"We've got nothing to say to the press, sorry."

"I'm not the press."

A man appeared from behind the counter.

"Who are you?" He eyed me suspiciously. "Are you sure, you're not the press?"

"I promise. My name is Jill Gooder. I'm a private investigator."

"What do you want?"

"My grandmother owns the wool shop just up the road."

"You mean Ever A Wool Moment?"

"You know it?"

"My gran is into knitting big time. She loves that shop and especially the Everlasting Wool."

"It was my grandmother who invented it. Look, the reason I'm here is that the police came to question her yesterday. Apparently, they're talking to all the local coffee shop and tea room owners. They have this crazy notion that the motive for the murder was to get Coffee Triangle closed down, and steal its customers."

He laughed. "You can't be serious. Surely, no one's going to commit murder just to put a rival out of business."

"I know. It's laughable. Anyway, it made her so angry that she's asked me to see what I can find out."

"Isn't that a job for the police?"

"You're right, but if my grandmother wants to pay me for trying to help, who am I to say no?"

"You're surely not taking money off your own flesh and blood?"

"Normally, I wouldn't. But this is Grandma. If you knew her, you'd understand."

"Fair enough, but I'm not sure I'll be able to help."

"Are you the manager?"

"Me? No. Tony's the manager. Tony Tuck. I'm the assistant manager. I'm Andy Tunow."

"Pleased to meet you, Andy. Is Tony around?"

"No, he's having a short break in Las Vegas."

"Really? Is he getting married?"

"No. Between you and me, Tony's a bit of a gambler. He likes to play the cards and have a bet on the horses. He reckons he's on a winning streak, so he's treated himself to a trip to the home of gambling."

"In that case, can *you* spare me a couple of minutes to answer a few questions?"

"Sure. Why not? There isn't much happening here until we open again. Come through to the back, and I'll make you a coffee."

The back office was quite large, but then it needed to be because it also acted as a store room for all the instruments.

"Wow! I didn't realise you had so many."

"Thirty tambourines, thirty triangles, thirty gongs, thirty drums. You name it, we've got thirty of them."

"It must have cost a pretty penny to set up."

"I'm sure it did, but it seems to have paid off. The place is busy most of the time. Drum day is our most popular day."

"I know. The last time I came here on drum day was with my young nephew. It was so busy that I only just managed to find a seat."

"Is he a drummer, your nephew?"

"Unfortunately, yes. Can you talk me through exactly what happened on the day of the murder?"

"There's not a lot to tell. It had been a normal day—much like any other. Then the woman who was sitting next to the murdered man realised he was dead, and screamed. It was pandemonium after that."

"Did anyone actually witness the murder?"

"No. At least not as far as I'm aware."

"What about the manager? Where was he while all this was going on?"

"I'm not sure. He'd been on the shop floor, playing a drum, for most of the shift."

"Playing a drum?"

"Yeah. He often leaves me to do the real work while he bangs a drum or shakes a tambourine."

"Did he call the police?"

"No—that was me. I don't actually know where Tony was—in the back having a crafty cigarette, probably. When the woman screamed, I dashed straight over to her, but I didn't see anything of Tony until after the police arrived."

"When does he get back from Vegas?"

"The day after tomorrow—just in time for when we reopen."

"Okay, well thanks for your time. I'll maybe pop in again then."

***

When I arrived at Cuppy C, I was quite surprised to find Amber sitting at a corner table with William. Neither of the twins seem to spend much time with their respective fiancés. Maybe the Sebastian incident had brought the twins to their senses?

"Hi, Jill." Amber spotted me.

"Hello, you two. Nice to see you again, William. I was beginning to think you were a figment of Amber's imagination."

He laughed. "I've been working all hours. I'm getting in as much overtime as I can."

"To keep Amber in dresses and shoes?"

"Don't say *that*, Jill." Amber protested, but she knew it was true. We both did.

"Where's Pearl?"

"Out shopping. It's fairly quiet in here today, so I said I'd watch the shop. And besides, William and I have important things to discuss."

"Oh, sorry. If you'd like me to leave you alone—"

"No, I didn't mean that. Come and sit with us. We've got something exciting to tell you."

'Exciting' could mean anything when it came to the twins. Still, I was curious enough to join them.

"You have to promise to keep it a secret," Amber said.

"You know me. I can keep a secret."

"Hmm?" Amber looked doubtful.

"I can. I won't tell anyone, I promise. Is it some juicy

gossip?"

"Nothing like that. One of the reasons William has been doing so much overtime is because we've been saving up."

"You have?" I hadn't seen much evidence of Amber saving. In fact, from what I'd seen, she'd been spending more money than ever on clothes, handbags, shoes, and jewellery.

"Yes, *I've* managed to save a little, but William has saved most of the money, haven't you, darling?"

William gave me a knowing look. I just bet he had. Ninety-nine percent of it, probably.

"Go on, then, Amber. Tell me what you've been saving up for."

"Shall we?" She looked at her fiancé.

"Sure, why not? I don't mind."

Amber looked around to make sure no one was listening. "You mustn't tell anyone, and you *definitely* mustn't tell Pearl."

"I won't. I promise."

"Or Mum."

"I'm not going to tell anyone. Now, what is it?"

"We've been house-hunting."

That was the last thing I'd expected her to say.

"House-hunting? You mean for you and William?"

"Of course. I can't wait to get away from Pearl. She drives me insane. You know what she's like."

I smiled. I knew what they were *both* like, and they were as bad as each other. I'd always thought it was strange that they'd chosen to live together because most of the time they fought like cat and dog. Even so, I hadn't seen this coming.

"When will you start looking at houses?"

"We've already found one."

"Already? Where is it?"

"It's only a couple of miles from Cuppy C, so I'll be able to walk to work every day. It's not too far from where William works, either. It's beautiful, Jill. Look." She took out her phone, clicked her way through a few screens, and then held it up for me to see.

The house in the photos did look lovely. Maybe a bit small, but that was to be expected for a first time buyer.

"Have you actually made an offer?"

"Not yet, but we're going to, aren't we, William?"

He nodded.

"Why don't you take a look at it, Jill?" Amber was so excited that she could barely sit still. "We'd love to know what you think, wouldn't we, William?"

"Me?" I said. "I don't really know much about houses."

"Maybe not, but you've got good taste."

That was so very true.

"Okay. If you give me the address, I'll pop over there when I get a chance."

***

The witnesses who'd come forward in the Coffee Triangle murder hadn't been named in the Bugle article, but a quick trip to the police station, combined with a little invisibility, had snagged me the names and contact details of all the people who had been in Coffee Triangle at the time of the incident. The four key witnesses—those who had been standing or sitting close to the murder victim— had been highlighted.

My first port of call was at Ridic Court; a block of flats very close to my own. I'd telephoned ahead and arranged to meet with an Adrienne Paige.

A woman, in her early thirties, answered the door.

"Adrienne? I'm Jill Gooder—I called earlier."

"Of course. Come in. Would you like a drink?"

"Do you have tea?"

"Sure. I don't have any biscuits though, I'm afraid."

"That's okay." Cheapskate. "Thank you for agreeing to see me."

"No problem. I'm between jobs at the moment, so it's not like I'm doing anything else."

When I stepped into the living room, it was as though someone had turned off the colour. Everything was either black or white.

Suddenly, something small and furry rushed past my feet. I almost jumped out of my skin. "What was that?"

"That's Stripe."

I looked all around the room—trying to catch another glimpse of Stripe. Then he dashed across the room and out of the door.

"He gets a little nervous around strangers." She passed me the tea.

"What is he?"

"Stripe? He's a skunk."

"Don't they make an awful smell?"

"Only if they feel threatened. Stripe's a little darling. Would you like to hold him?"

"No thanks, I'm good." The tea tasted like Stripe had made it. "I guess a Zebra would be too big?" I laughed.

Adrienne looked confused.

"I assume you got Stripe to match the décor?"

She glanced around, and then smiled. "That had never occurred to me. I suppose he is a good match. No, I've always kept skunks—ever since I was a kid. I tried a dog once, but there wasn't the same connection."

"Thank you for agreeing to talk to me. I understand you were sitting quite close to the man who was murdered?"

"I was actually standing. I couldn't get a seat, so I was leaning on the end of the booth where he was sitting."

"Did you see the shooting? Or hear the shot?"

"I didn't see anyone shoot him, and it was too noisy to hear yourself think. From what I understand, no one actually saw the shooting."

"Can you tell me what you *did* see?"

"I thought the woman in the seat opposite him was getting ready to leave. I was keeping an eye on her, so I'd be able to grab her seat. The woman next to the murder victim was getting more and more annoyed because he'd left her hardly any room. I think she said something to him, but he didn't respond. She must have nudged his arm to get his attention, and he fell, head first onto the table."

"What happened then?"

"It took a few seconds for people to realise what had happened. They probably thought he was just drunk, and had passed out. Then someone shouted, 'There's blood', and everyone looked around. There was blood all over the table. Then people started screaming and shouting."

We spoke for a short while longer. She more or less confirmed what Andy Tunow had already told me. On my way out, I caught another glimpse of Stripe—fortunately for me, he didn't feel threatened.

The next woman on my list was Joy Sanders. She lived in a terraced house on Ulous Road. Joy had been less enthusiastic about talking to me, but in the end, I'd managed to convince her to spare me a few minutes.

"Have you been collecting these long?" I was transfixed by the display of egg-timers.

"I don't collect them. I hate the stupid things."

"Oh?"

"They belong to my mother. She has so many that she's run out of space in her house. Like an idiot, I said she could leave a few of them here. That was three years ago. It started with five of them, and now I've got almost as many here as she has at her place. I wouldn't mind, but she expects me to dust them."

"Oh dear."

"That's not the worst part. She insists that I turn them over four times a day. According to her, the sand gets lumpy otherwise."

"That must be a bit of a pain."

"It is, but between you and me—" She looked around as though expecting someone else to be listening. "I only do it twice a day."

"That's understandable. Anyway, thanks for sparing me the time. I believe you were sitting next to the victim?"

"Yes, I was. The big stupid oaf." She hesitated. "I probably shouldn't say that now he's dead, should I? He was taking up almost one and a half seats; I only just managed to squeeze on. I thought that once I sat down, he'd shuffle along a bit, but he didn't. He just sat there; he never budged—I guess that's because he was dead."

"Could he have been dead when you sat down?"

"I don't know; it's possible. He didn't speak and he didn't move, so maybe he was. I hadn't been sitting there long myself."

"You didn't see or hear a shot after you sat down?"

"No. It was only when I got fed up, and tried to get him to shuffle along that he fell head first onto the table. It scared me to death. And the blood ruined my skirt."

"So you've got no idea who might have done it?"

"None at all. I didn't see anything. I don't think anyone did." She checked her watch. "Look, if there's nothing else, it's time for me to turn all of these over."

"Would you like a hand?"

"That would be great. Do you mind?"

"Not at all. It's the least I can do."

I spoke to the other two key witnesses, and they told a similar story. No one had actually seen anything, and no one had heard the gunshot because of the noise from the drums. The first anyone had known about the murder was when the man had fallen head first onto the table.

I was getting nowhere fast.

Chapter 15

Custard cream nirvana! Oh yeah!

I'd just bought a brand new packet, and I had the whole evening to myself. Of course, I'd have to regulate my consumption of the aforementioned custard creams. I definitely wouldn't eat more than four of them—maybe five—six at the very most.

I'd only just settled down on the sofa when there was a knock at the door. Please don't let it be Betty or Mr Ivers.

It was Horace. He really was a mountain of a man, and seemed even bigger now that he was standing directly in front of me.

"Horace? Is Grandma with you?"

"No. I'm alone. I hope you don't mind me calling on you like this, unannounced."

"Err. No. Of course not."

"May I come in?"

"Sorry. Yes, of course. Would you like a cup of tea? Or coffee?"

"Nothing for me, thanks." He looked around the living room, and for the longest moment, a silence seemed to hang in the air.

"Do you have relatives or friends in Washbridge, Horace?" I felt the need to break the awkward silence.

"No."

"Business interests?"

"No. I spend as little time as possible in the human world." He was staring straight at me now. "Why do *you* insist on living among *humans*, Jill?"

The question caught me completely off guard, and I was a little surprised by how much venom the word 'humans' seemed to carry.

"This is where I was raised. It's all I knew until recently."

"Don't you feel vulnerable?"

I was beginning to.

"Not at all. Are you sure you wouldn't like a drink?"

"No, thank you. Your grandmother tells me that you're going to be the first level seven witch."

Grandma said that? I was astonished.

"I'm not sure about that. I've still got a lot to learn." My nervous laugh gave away just how uncomfortable I was beginning to feel.

"I sense a force within you, Jill. It's very powerful."

I had absolutely no idea how to respond to that.

"A force like that shouldn't be wasted." His eyes were burning into me.

"Look," I said. "I don't want to be rude, but my sister is coming over." I glanced at my watch. "Anytime now."

"Kathy? How is she?"

"Very well, thanks." How did he know Kathy's name? Had Grandma told him? Probably.

"And those darling children, Mikey and Lizzie?" Horace continued. "Children are such a precious gift. Be sure to tell Kathy to look out for them. Danger lurks everywhere."

"Sorry?"

"I won't keep you." He started for the door. "I'll see you again soon, I'm sure."

When he'd gone, I felt—I don't know—dirty. What was that all about? I checked the door, to make sure it was locked. Then, I double-checked the French doors, too.

I'd lost my appetite—even for custard creams.

***

The next morning, I felt pretty ropey. I hadn't slept well. I kept waking up and thinking about Horace's surprise visit, and in particular his mention of Kathy and the kids. It was probably harmless. Of course it was harmless. He was just a little strange, but then he'd have to be to put up with Grandma.

Very little had been said in The Bugle about the murder victim other than his name: Joe Snow. And his occupation: an accountant. I'd tried to get hold of Tom Hawk to see if he could give me any more details, but he was either too busy to return my calls or he was ignoring me.

It didn't take long to find an address for Snow's accountancy practice. I was surprised to see that it was located in the seedier part of Washbridge. Accountants, solicitors and other professionals tended to have their offices in the more prestigious parts of the city centre.

As I'd expected, the building where Joe Snow's office was located was fairly run down, and occupied mostly by small start-ups. His office was locked, and I was still trying to decide what to do when the door to the next office opened, and out walked a very tall man. He was at least six feet six, slim, and was wearing blue overalls stained with what I hoped was red ink.

"Are you looking for Joe?"

"Actually, no. I understand he was killed."

"That's right. Very strange affair. I read he got shot in that coffee shop; the one where they play triangles and drums."

"Did you know him? Sorry, what's your name?"

"Les Winters. We'd said 'hello' a few times. That's all. He was never here."

"How do you mean?"

"Between you and me, this isn't really his office."

"It's the address given for his accountancy business."

He glanced around in case anyone was listening. "He wasn't really an accountant."

"How do you mean? What *did* he do then?"

"I don't suppose it matters if I tell you now. I only found out by chance. He was actually a — what would you call it? A loan shark. He lent money to people. The interest rates he charged were ridiculous. Just out of curiosity, I once asked him about borrowing some money. I could do with a new printing press, but not at the rates he was charging. He always seemed pleasant enough, but from what I understand, he could be a nasty piece of work. He was okay if you paid on time, but if you didn't, you were in big trouble. He had a reputation for violence."

"You said this isn't really his office. Does that mean he had another office somewhere else?"

"I shouldn't really say."

"He's hardly going to complain now, is he?"

"That's true. He did once ask me to forward some mail to him. I have the address in my office, I think. Would you like me to go and look for it?"

"Yes, please. If you don't mind."

He disappeared back inside. So, Joe Snow had been a loan shark with a reputation for violence. This was becoming more and more interesting.

"There you go." The man passed me a slip of paper. "You won't tell anybody I gave it to you, will you?"

"My lips are sealed."

Joe Snow's real office was in downtown Washbridge. A much more upmarket area than the office I'd just visited. This building was very modern, and had a security guard at the desk on the ground floor.

If I walked nonchalantly by, maybe the security guard would assume I worked in one of the offices.

"Excuse me, madam. Excuse me!"

Drat!

"Me?"

"Yes, you. Where are you going?"

"To room three-one-eight."

"Where's your ID badge?"

"I left it on my desk."

"Sorry, madam. No ID, no entry."

"But I need to get back to the office."

"You'll have to phone them, and get someone to bring your badge down to you."

"But I'll be late."

"Sorry, madam. There's nothing I can do about that."

The man wasn't to be moved, but while we were talking, I noticed a number of photographs on the wall behind him. One of them was of the manager of the building, another was of the Assistant Manager, and the final one was of the Head of Security. I memorised the latter's face, made an excuse, and then left the building.

I waited for a few minutes before casting the 'doppelganger' spell which made me look like the Head of Security. This time, when I walked toward the desk, I got a very different reaction from the security guard.

"Good afternoon, Mr Carruthers." He practically saluted me. "I had no idea you were coming in today."

"I like to pay a surprise visit from time to time. Keeps the staff on their toes. How are things?"

"Everything's fine, sir. Absolutely fine."

"Are you sure about that?"

"Yes, sir. No problems at all."

"Good. Well you won't mind if I have a quick look around, then?"

"No, sir. I'll accompany you."

"I'd rather do it alone. You stay here. I'll let you know if anything's not to my liking."

"Yes, sir. Certainly, sir."

That was easier than I'd expected. Once in the lift, I reversed the spell.

The door to room three-one-eight was locked. After I'd checked that the coast was clear, I cast the 'power' spell, and forced the door open—breaking the lock as I did. Once inside, I cast the 'take it back' spell to return the lock to its original state.

The office was practically bare. There was a single leather chair, a metal desk, and behind those, a filing cabinet. I'd expected to find a computer, but there was nothing of that nature.

I tried the drawers of the filing cabinet; they weren't locked. Presumably Joe Snow didn't expect anyone to find his office, and certainly not to get past security, and through a locked door. The top drawer was empty. There were a few books in the middle drawer, but nothing of any interest. The bottom drawer contained a single large book; it was some sort of ledger.

I flicked through the pages. This was obviously where Joe Snow kept his record of debtors and payments. He presumably didn't trust computers or the internet. It was all very old-school; all hand written. I flicked through to the letter 'T', and soon found what I was looking for: Tony Tuck, the manager of Coffee Triangle. And it didn't make pretty reading. Tony had borrowed twelve thousand pounds, and although I was no accountant, it appeared that his payments were way overdue. When Tony Tuck realised that he couldn't make the payments, he must have feared for his safety because, if Les Winters was to be believed, Joe Snow could be a violent man.

But even if that was motive enough for Tony Tuck to commit murder, it didn't explain how he'd done it. And more importantly, where was the murder weapon? Without that, I had nothing.

***

I decided to take a look at the house that Amber and William were thinking of buying. Just as Amber had said, it wasn't far from Cuppy C. From the outside, at least, it was delightful, but I'd forgotten to ask Amber where I could get hold of the key to take a look inside.

I walked around to the back of the house, and took a look through one of the windows. The kitchen looked very new, but I doubted Amber would be doing much cooking. On a whim, I tried the back door, and to my surprise, it opened. I knew the house wasn't occupied because Amber had told me that it was vacant possession. The previous owner had moved to the human world. So, why was the door unlocked?

It couldn't do any harm to take a quick look inside.

I walked through the kitchen into a small hallway. The carpet was horrible; a swirl of red, brown and green—not exactly easy on the eye. But that could easily be replaced. Amber had mentioned that the previous owner had left some furniture in the living room, which was going to be included in the sale. No wonder they were leaving it behind; it was ghastly.

Just then, I heard footsteps and voices coming from upstairs. Whoops! It hadn't occurred to me that someone else might be looking around the house. That would explain the unlocked door. Then I heard footsteps on the stairs. I had to get out before they saw me. I was almost at the back door when I heard a familiar voice.

"Jill? Is that you?"

I turned around to see Pearl and Alan; they both looked rather puzzled.

"What are *you* doing here?" Pearl said. "How did you know we were here?"

"Err—I—"

"Does Amber know we're here?"

"No, I don't think so."

"You mustn't tell her."

"Okay."

"So how *did* you know we were here?"

"I didn't. I was just viewing houses."

"Are you looking for a house in Candlefield too?"

"Not seriously. Not at the moment, anyway. I'm quite happy with the flat above Cuppy C, but I was at a bit of a loose end, so I thought I'd check out the local housing market. Just in case I do decide to buy one day."

"Well, you can't have this house." Pearl grinned. "We love it. Don't we, Alan?"

"Yes, we do."

"Hi, Alan," I said. "I haven't seen you for a while."

"I've been busy working lots of overtime."

"We've been saving up." Pearl put her arm through Alan's. "We've been planning to get our own house for ages. I can't wait to get away from Amber. She drives me insane. You know what she's like, Jill."

I smiled. The irony.

"You mustn't say anything to her. We don't want her to know that we've bought the house until it's all sorted. You won't say anything, will you?"

"Of course not. Are you going to put in an offer for this place?"

"Yes, it's the best one we've seen by a long chalk, isn't it Alan?"

"Yes. Best by far."

"You're not thinking of putting in an offer too, are you, Jill?" Pearl looked a little worried.

"No. Definitely not."

"That's good. We'd hate to lose out to someone else."

"That would be horrible," I agreed. "Look, I've got to dash. Things to do. I promised Barry I'd take him for a walk. I'll see you both soon."

"Okay, and please don't tell Amber, will you? Or Mum. Don't tell anyone."

"My lips are sealed." I ran my fingers across my lips and zipped them closed.

Oh dear. This wasn't going to end well.

Chapter 16

I had a hunch, but it was a long shot; a really long shot. And, I didn't want to show my hand until I was sure. I still had the list of names and contact details for all the people who had been in Coffee Triangle that day. The police had spoken to everyone on the list, but most of them hadn't been able to help because they weren't anywhere near the incident.

It took me the best part of three hours to call everyone on the list—I had just one question for them all. Even though there were a few people I didn't manage to get hold of, it didn't matter because I was able to identify thirty people who'd had a drum at the moment when the murder victim was found. The assistant manager at Coffee Triangle had told me there were thirty of each of the instruments, which meant that at the moment the murder victim was found, every drum in the shop was accounted for. So, if thirty customers had drums, where had the manager got his from? And where was he when the victim was discovered? According to the assistant manager, his boss had been on the shop floor, playing his drum for most of the day. And yet, when the body was discovered, the assistant manager was forced to step in because the manager couldn't be found.

Where had he gone?

Tony Tuck owed money to the murdered man, and payment was long overdue. From all accounts, Joe Snow wasn't the kind of man you wanted to cross. So, why had Joe Snow been in Coffee Triangle that day? Was he there to collect his money? Was he there to intimidate Tuck? Or had the situation moved beyond intimidation? Was Snow there to deal out some kind of punishment? It was unlikely to have been a social call.

Maybe the manager had feared for his life, and decided to get in first. He certainly had the motive, but if he was the killer, the big question was how did he do it? No one had seen or heard the gunshot, and although the police had searched the premises, no murder weapon had been found. All my instincts told me that if I could find the weapon, everything else would fall into place.

Easier said than done.

***

I needed to clear my head and stop obsessing over the Coffee Triangle case, so I magicked myself over to Candlefield.

Amber had gone out to visit one of the cake suppliers.

"Hey, Jill." Pearl greeted me. "I have news."

"What's that?"

"You won't tell Amber, will you?"

"No. I promise."

"You know we were looking around that house the other day?"

"Yeah."

"And you know we said we might make an offer on it?"

"I remember."

"Well, we did. And we should hear back sometime today. With a bit of luck, Alan and I could soon have our very own house. I'll be able to move out and leave Amber behind."

"Did the estate agent say that you were in with a good chance?"

"They were being a bit cagey, but we think so. They said at least two other couples had shown an interest, but we were the first to put in an offer. So now we're just waiting to hear if the seller has accepted it. I'm really excited. I can't wait to have our own place. I know exactly how we'll decorate it. We're going to paint it yellow throughout."

"Every room?"

"Yeah, I like yellow. And we'll have a nice blue carpet in the living room, and a yellow and blue corner sofa."

"Hmm? A lot of yellow and blue then?"

"Yeah. We might have to wait a while for the rest of the furniture because we won't have a lot of money left after we've paid the deposit for the house."

Later, when Amber got back, she joined me behind the counter while Pearl went on her break.

"Hey, Jill. I have something to tell you, but you mustn't tell anyone; particularly not Pearl."

I had a horrible feeling I knew what was coming.

"Sure, what is it?"

"You know the house that William and me have been looking at?"

"Yeah."

"Well, we decided to put in an offer."

"You did? Have you heard back yet?"

"No, but the estate agent said they'd contact us today. I'm expecting a phone call anytime, so fingers crossed. I can't wait to get out of this place, and away from Pearl. We already know exactly how we'll decorate it."

"Let me guess. You're going to paint it yellow throughout?"

"No. Why would we do that? We're going to paint it blue throughout."

"Blue? Right."

"And we're going to have a yellow carpet in the living room."

"And a yellow and blue sofa?"

"How did you know?"

"Just a lucky guess."

"That's all the furniture we'll be able to afford to begin with because we won't have much money left after we've paid the deposit for the house."

About an hour later, Pearl, Amber and I were sitting at a window table. Somebody had forced me to have a blueberry muffin. We hadn't been there for more than a few minutes when a phone rang, and then another phone rang. Pearl and Amber both jumped up from their seats, and dashed to opposite sides of the room. I glanced back and forth between the two of them, wondering which one of them had got the house. But when they'd finished on their calls, and returned to the table, they both had long faces.

"Everything okay?" I said.

"Fine." Amber sighed.

"Just great." Pearl frowned.

Later on, I caught up with Amber when she was by herself. "I guess that was bad news on the house front?"

"Yeah, somebody put in a better offer. It's been sold."

"Oh well, never mind. There'll be plenty more."

"I guess so. But we had our heart set on that one."

I had the same conversation with Pearl ten minutes later. Little did they know, they'd both put in a bid for the same house. In a way, this was the best possible outcome. Someone else had bought the house. If Amber had got it, Pearl would have gone ballistic. If Pearl had got it, Amber would have killed her. And I would have been stuck in the middle of it all.

The atmosphere in the shop over the next couple of hours wasn't great. Neither Amber nor Pearl was in the mood for talking. Ironically, I was the only one who knew why both of them were so downcast. Amber had a go at Pearl for being moody. Pearl accused Amber of being a misery guts.

"What are those two up to over there?" Pearl said.

Amber and I both followed her gaze.

"What on earth are they doing?" Amber had her nose pressed to the window.

It was Miles Best and Mindy Lowe.

"It looks like they're dancing." Pearl shook her head. "Knowing their luck, they've probably won the lottery."

I was intrigued. So much so, that I volunteered to go over the road to find out what was happening.

"Hello, Jill!" Miles shouted when he saw me.

"What's going on? Have you managed to shut down another cake shop with your rats?"

"That was only a bit of fun. You and the twins really shouldn't take things so seriously."

I was *so* tempted to slap the smile off his face.

"So why are you dancing in the street?"

He couldn't wait to tell me.

"So?" Amber said when I walked back into Cuppy C. "What are they up to?"

"Have they won the lottery?" Pearl was still staring at the crazy, dancing couple.

"It's nothing." I shrugged.

"It must be something." Amber insisted. "They wouldn't be dancing in the street like lunatics for no reason."

"Honestly, it's nothing."

"Jill!" Pearl glared at me. "Tell us."

"Well if you must know. They've just found out that the offer they put in on a house has been accepted."

All three of us knew which house it was.

***

There was nothing I could say which would make the twins feel any better, so I waited until the shop was quiet, said my goodbyes, and headed back to Washbridge.

When I got to the office, Mrs V was standing behind her desk. There was a large box in front of her, and she appeared to be emptying her drawers.

"Mrs V, what's going on?"

"As if you care."

Her reaction completely floored me.

"What do you mean?"

"I resign."

"Resign? But why?"

"I thought I could trust you, Jill. I thought you were my friend."

"I *am* your friend. And, of course you can trust me. What's happened?"

She took a deep breath. I could tell she was barely holding back the tears.

"I'm under investigation by the local chapter of the Yarnies."

"Under investigation? Whatever for?"

"Someone told them—" She had to take a deep breath to get the words out. "Someone told them that I've been crocheting."

I laughed, but immediately realised that was the wrong reaction. "Sorry, sorry."

"It's not funny. It's not funny at all. I don't understand why you would tell someone."

"Me? I haven't told anyone. You asked me not to say anything, and I haven't."

"Who else could it have been?"

"I don't know, but it definitely wasn't me. Please don't leave, Mrs V. We've been together for so long. You have to believe me. I haven't told anyone. At least let me investigate, and try to get to the bottom of it."

She hesitated. "I suppose I owe you that much."

"So, you'll stay?"

"Yes, but only if you promise to find out who did it."

"Don't worry. I'll find out."

If Winky was responsible for this, I would kill him. Slowly and very painfully.

He was on the sofa.

"How could you do it?"

He looked confused. "How could I do what?"

"You told someone about Mrs V crocheting."

"Do me a favour. I have much better things to do with my time than worry about the old bag lady, and what kind of needles she's using."

"You said you were going to post it on FelineSocial."

"I was only kidding. I wouldn't waste my time."

"I don't believe you." I grabbed his phone.

"Hey! What do you think you're doing? That's private."

"I don't care."

I soon found the FelineSocial app, and clicked on it.

"Hey, do you mind? Stop reading my personal stuff."

I scrolled all the way down. There was no mention of Mrs V or crocheting.

"Now do you believe me?" he said, as indignantly as he could.

"Yeah. Here." I passed him the phone.

"No apology then?"

"I'm sorry."

"That hardly covers it. Still, there is one way you can make it up to me."

"Salmon?"

"Red not pink, obviously."

Chapter 17

"What exactly is it I'm paying you for?" Grandma had just burst into my office—leaving Mrs V in her wake. "There isn't much sign of you finding out who the Coffee Triangle murderer is."

"I'm working on it."

"Really? Because from where I'm standing, it looks like you're categorising your rubber bands. How much is that costing me?"

I opened the top drawer of my desk, and swept the rubber bands inside.

"They help me to think."

"Oh, well that's okay then. I don't mind paying you to play with your rubber bands just as long as it helps you to think."

"I've told you I'm working on the case. I expect to have a result soon."

"You'd better have." And with that she left.

No pressure then.

The Coffee Triangle case was really beginning to bug me, and not just because I had Grandma on my back. I was missing something obvious, but what? It was too much of a coincidence that the victim, Joe Snow, just happened to be in the shop. Tony Tuck had owed him money, and my gut feeling was that Snow had been there to collect. Either his money or his pound of flesh. Tuck must have known he was in trouble, and decided to get in first.

But how had he done it? It was obvious why no one had heard the gunshot, but why had no one seen him with a gun, and where was the murder weapon now? I knew from what his assistant had told me, that the manager had gone AWOL for a few minutes around the time the victim was found. I definitely wasn't going to find the gun sitting at my desk, so I made my way down to Coffee Triangle.

If my hunch about Tuck was correct, he couldn't have gone far in such a short period of time. At the back of the building was a high wall, but that didn't pose an obstacle; I simply levitated over it. I was really getting the hang of levitation now.

There was very little to see in the yard behind Coffee Triangle, but I did notice that the area was shared by three adjoining shops. All of them had back doors which opened onto the yard. Tuck would have had time to come out of Coffee Triangle, and nip into one of those, but which one?

Then it struck me. Why hadn't I thought of it before? Two doors down from Coffee Triangle was Tom Tom Music — where Mikey had spent an hour playing on their drum kits. Where better to hide a drum than in plain sight in a music shop?

But I still had to find it.

I made my way back to the front of the building. The music shop was deserted except for the two men behind the counter.

"Morning," I said.

"Morning." The taller of the two men flashed me a smile. He had a gold front tooth. "Weren't you in here the other day?"

"Yeah. With my young nephew." I walked over to the counter.

"That's right. I remember now. Quite the budding

drummer. I'm Tom."

"Jill. Pleased to meet you."

"I'm Tom two." The second man had a tattoo of a cow playing a banjo on his upper arm.

"Tom and Tom? Doesn't that get confusing?"

"Not really. He's Tom, and I'm Tom Number Two."

"Ah, right. Tom *Two*. I thought you said Tom *too*."

They both looked confused now.

"So, did your nephew find a drum kit he liked?" Tom Two said.

"He liked them all. He's hoping to get one for his birthday."

"He's welcome to come down and try them out any time."

"Thanks. I'll tell his mum." She'll be so pleased.

"What brings you here today?" Tom asked. "Are you looking for something in particular?"

"I'm a private investigator. I assume you heard about the murder at the coffee shop a couple of doors away."

"Terrible business," Tom said. "On a purely selfish note, I hope it doesn't damage their business long term."

"Selfish how?"

"That shop has been really good for us. They buy all their instruments from here."

"You'll know Tony Tuck, then?"

"Yeah. He's always in here. Those instruments take some hammer."

"I hadn't thought of that. So, I assume he comes in quite often to order new ones?"

"Yeah. Plus, he leaves all the damaged ones with us. We're able to repair some of them."

"Where do you keep the damaged instruments he

brings in?"

"There's a storeroom over there." Tom pointed. "Tony brings them through the door from the common yard at the back."

"Can I take a look?"

"Sure. Knock yourself out."

The store room was a mess. There were damaged instruments of every kind scattered all over the floor—this was going to take a while. I had to approach it logically, so I started from the left hand side of the room, checking each drum I came across. I was about two thirds of the way through them when I spotted a drum with a tear in its skin.

Just as I'd suspected, there was something inside it.

***

Tony Tuck wouldn't be back from Vegas for at least another day. In the meantime, I had to make good on my promise to find out who'd let Mrs V's secret out of the bag.

One of Armitage's people, maybe? But how would they have known? Mrs V definitely wouldn't have taken out her crochet while they were there. Someone must have been through her drawers, but who else had access to her desk?

And then it struck me! Of course!

I gave Kathy a call, and just as I hoped, she had the address I needed.

Doreen Daggers greeted me with a smile.

"Jill. Do come in. How did you know where I lived?"

"My sister, Kathy, found your address in the Ever members' database. I hope you don't mind?"

"Not at all. It's lovely to see you. I don't get many visitors."

I followed her through to the lounge.

"Can I get you a drink?"

"No thanks, Doreen. Look, there's something I need to ask you."

"I think I know what it is. Me and my big mouth. I just don't know when to keep quiet."

"You told the Yarnies about Mrs V's crochet?"

"Not intentionally. I spotted it when I was looking for a tissue in V's desk. It didn't bother me at all. I've never understood why there's so much animosity between the knitters and the crocheters. But like an idiot, I let it slip in front of Phyllis Cartwright, Vice President of the local Yarnies. I could have kicked myself. As soon as I'd said it, I knew I'd made a terrible mistake. I couldn't bring myself to tell Annabel. She's been such a good friend to me over the years. I suppose you'll have to tell her now though."

"Maybe, maybe not. But I will need Phyllis Cartwright's address."

I arrived on Phyllis Cartwright's doorstep unannounced. She was all doilies and lace curtains.

"Yes? Who are you?" she said, while trying not to swallow the plum in her mouth.

"I'm Jill Gooder. I'm a private investigator. I believe you know my P.A, Annabel Versailles?"

"Yes, I know Annabel. Now, what can I do for you, young lady?"

"It's more a case of what I can do for you. I'm here to

save you from embarrassing yourself. May I come in?" I didn't wait for a reply; I just stepped inside.

"What do you mean? Why would I embarrass myself? Why exactly are you here, Miss Gooder?"

I put my bag on the coffee table, and took from it first a small trophy, and then a framed photo. "Please take a close look at these."

She picked up the cup and read the inscription, and then checked the caption on the photo.

"*You're* the regional crochet champion?"

"Third year in a row, actually. So, you see, I keep crochet all over my office, including some in Mrs V's desk. She doesn't like it, but she's my employee, so she has to put up with it. Now, from what she tells me, you've accused her of being in possession of crochet."

"That was the information I was given." Her air of confidence had evaporated.

"Well, it seems you were misled, and if you insist on pursuing this, I'll be forced to come forward to clarify matters. I don't think that would look very good for you."

"There's no need for that. Now I've been made aware of the situation, no further action will be taken, obviously."

"I knew you would see sense."

"Thank you so much, Jill," Mrs V said. She was full of smiles when I got back to the office. "The Yarnies Vice President just phoned to say that they won't be pursuing the crochet incident."

"That's great."

"I'm very sorry I doubted you."

"Don't give it a second thought."

"Doreen called earlier too. She told me that she was the

one who had let it slip."

"I hope you weren't too hard on her."

"Of course not. She and I go way back. I know she wouldn't have done it maliciously. All's well that ends well. Oh, and by the way, Jill, you must show me your crochet trophies sometime."

***

Thank goodness I'd persuaded Mrs V to stay. Even though she did very little 'real' work, the office simply wouldn't have been the same without her. To reward myself for a job well done, I decided coffee and a blueberry muffin were in order. Coffee Triangle was still closed, so I tried another coffee shop — one I hadn't been in before: Beans.

As soon as I walked through the door, I realised that I'd been wrong when I'd assumed the shop's name referred to coffee *beans*.

"Yes, madam." A bubbly, young woman behind the counter greeted me. She had a fringe which made her look a little like an Old English Sheepdog. "What can I get for you?"

"A regular latte, please. And a muffin of the blueberry persuasion, I think."

I was still trying to figure out how I was going to balance the latte while sitting on one of the dozens of bean bags spread across the floor.

"Jill!" someone called.

It was Hilary; one of the girls from Love Spell.

"Come and join me." She patted the bean bag next to hers.

I somehow managed to lower myself onto the red and white striped bean bag without spilling my drink.

"Do you come in here often?" I said.

"This is only my second time. I usually go to Coffee Triangle."

"Me too. I miss the tambourines."

"Still they do have bean bags here. Lots of them."

"Is it just me or is this a weird idea?"

"It's totally weird. I've seen three people spill their drinks in the last twenty minutes."

"How's the dating business?"

"Going from strength to strength. We can't find enough human men to keep up with demand."

"Mr Ivers doesn't seem to be having much luck."

"No, we're still trying to find him a match, but we get the same feedback from every witch he dates."

"Too boring?"

"Got it in one."

Just then, someone pulled up a bean bag next to ours. It was Jim Keeper, the Grim Reaper. Instinctively, both Hilary and I made to stand up.

"Don't leave ladies, please. Just give me a moment."

Hilary and I exchanged a worried look.

"I'm not on duty," he said. "There's nothing to worry about."

"What do you want, Jim?" I asked.

"Just some advice. It was actually you I wanted to see, Hilary."

"In that case I'll be off," I said.

"No!" Hilary grabbed my arm. "Please stay, Jill." I could see the terror in her eyes.

"Okay then."

"Look, ladies," Jim said. "You know I've been having a lot of difficulty with finding a partner." He turned to me. "*You* dumped me after just one date."

What could I say? It was true.

"And you, Hilary. *You* threw me off your books."

"We only allow human men to register."

"It's okay," he said. "I'm used to it. No one wants to know a Grim Reaper. I feel like we've had some bad press."

"What was it you wanted to see me about?" Hilary sounded nervous.

"It suddenly occurred to me that I can't be the only Reaper with this problem. So I got to thinking. Why don't I start my own dating agency—just for Reapers? I could call it Grim Cupid or Love you to Death."

"I think you'll need to work on the name," I said.

"You could be right. Anyway, Hilary, I was hoping you might give me some advice, based on your experience. You know: tips, pitfalls to watch out for; that kind of thing."

"Sure. Why not?" Hilary seemed to have relaxed a little.

"Right," I struggled to my feet. "I really do have to go now. Good luck with your new venture, Jim."

When I reached the door, I turned back to them. "How about 'Reap the Love'?"

Chapter 18

Coffee Triangle was scheduled to reopen at nine a.m. When I arrived there at seven-thirty, the lights were on, so I knew someone was inside. I banged on the door, and eventually Tony Tuck, the manager, appeared from the back office.

"We're not open yet," he shouted.

I banged on the door again.

"Nine o'clock!"

I banged on the door again.

He was clearly annoyed as he approached the door. "We're not open!"

"Let me in. I have something I need to talk to you about."

"It'll have to wait until nine o'clock."

"This can't wait. I want to talk to you about Joe Snow."

"You can't come in."

"Unlock the door or I'll break it down."

He looked more puzzled than worried, but he unlocked the door anyway.

"Who are you? What's this about?"

"My name is Jill Gooder. I'm a private investigator."

"If you have information about the murder, you should take it to the police."

"Don't worry, I will, but first I want to know why you killed Snow."

"What are you talking about?"

"I know you owed him money. Had he threatened to harm you? Or kill you? Is that why you did it?"

"You're talking nonsense. Get out of here before I call the police."

"Why don't you do that? I'm sure they'd be interested to hear what I have to tell them."

"I don't know what you're talking about. I didn't kill anybody. You can't prove a thing."

"That's where you're wrong. I'm fairly sure that once the police examine the murder weapon, they'll be able to trace it back to you one way or another."

"What murder weapon? There is no murder weapon. The police said they couldn't find it. Get out of here before I throw you out." He started towards me, but I easily pushed him away. The 'power' spell made me far stronger than he was.

He looked surprised. "You can't prove anything," he repeated. "You're wasting your time."

"Hmm. Well, let's see now. This is what I think happened. Joe Snow came around to collect on his debt. He probably threatened to hurt or even kill you, but when he got here the shop was absolutely packed. He couldn't do anything while there were people around, so he took a seat and waited. You knew what was going to happen after everyone had left. Things were going to turn nasty. The drums had already been handed out, but you knew that there were plenty of damaged ones down at Tom Tom. You'd probably had the gun for some time because you were expecting trouble. This was your opportunity. You hid the gun in the drum until you were standing right next to Snow. No one saw you shoot him—you made sure of that by standing in such a way that the drum obscured the view of those close by. And no one heard anything because there was so much noise in the shop at the time. Then you slid the gun back inside the drum, and took it back to Tom Tom. You knew that the drums waiting for repair could be there for weeks or even months. You no doubt planned to dispose of it once things had quietened down. How am I doing so far?"

Tuck had turned pale; he obviously knew the game was up. He rushed forward, and tried to push me out of the way, but I easily deflected him, and then used the 'tie-up' spell to bind his feet and hands.

"What are you going to do now?" he said, panic-stricken.

"That's for the police to decide. It's possible you may get off with a lesser charge once they know Snow had threatened you."

I fetched the drum, with the gun still inside it, from my car, and put it on the floor next to him. Then I made a call to Tom Hawk.

***

Aunt Lucy had phoned to ask if I'd go straight over to see her.

"Thanks for coming over, Jill. I made some muffins yesterday, would you like to try one?"

"What flavour are they?"

"Your favourite, blueberry."

"Go on then, if you're twisting my arm."

Aunt Lucy made tea for us both. The muffin was delicious. Maybe I should have had two?

"Why did you want to see me, Aunt Lucy. Is everything okay?"

"Yeah—everything's fine. I suppose."

"That's not very convincing."

"It's just that I've had a bit of a shock."

"What's happened?"

"Yesterday, out of the blue, Lester suddenly suggested that he'd like us to live in the human world."

For some reason, I'd never pictured Aunt Lucy living anywhere other than Candlefield. In fact, I couldn't imagine her living anywhere other than in that house.

"What brought that up?"

"Lester used to live and work in the human world, but it's quite a long time ago now."

"I didn't know that."

"He worked as a traffic warden. He's always saying how much he enjoyed the job, and how friendly the people were."

"Are you sure he said 'traffic warden'?"

"Positive. He said people were always happy to see him."

Lester was either delusional or he'd had a drink problem back then.

"Anyway," Aunt Lucy continued. "He came out with the idea yesterday; completely out of the blue. It was the last thing I'd expected him to suggest."

"Have you ever lived in the human world?"

"No. I've never really had any desire to. I've been there many times, but never to stay. Not even for a single night. I've always lived here in Candlefield, among sups. It's where I feel comfortable. It's where I belong."

"What did you say to him?"

"I said I couldn't give him an answer straight away. That I'd need time to think about it. And, to be fair, he understood."

"Have you told anyone else about this—what about Grandma?"

"No. Your grandmother wouldn't like the idea at all. She's not a fan of the human world."

"But *she* has a business in Washbridge."

"Yeah, but it's a case of *'Do as I say, not do as I do'* with Grandma. You should know that by now."

It was true. Grandma was always telling me I should live in Candlefield, and yet she spent almost as much time in Washbridge as I did.

"What about the twins? Haven't you told them either?"

"No. I need to think this through for myself first. I know both of them would love to move to the human world one day, but it's not really practical at the moment. Not while they have Cuppy C to run. I'm not sure how they'd cope if I moved there."

"They're grown women, Aunt Lucy. They should be able to take care of themselves."

"You'd think so, wouldn't you, but judging by the amount of time they spend around here, the number of things they ask me to do for them, and the amount of money they borrow from me—"

"I didn't know they borrowed money from you. They shouldn't need to do that—they have their own business."

"I know, but have you seen how many clothes they buy? Those two girls have never been any different. If I moved to the human world, how would they cope? Anyway, I just wanted to ask if you had any thoughts on it."

"Not really. Maybe you could try spending a few days there. That would give you a chance to see whether you'd like to live there or not."

"That's a good idea. I could spend a little time there between now and the wedding. Then, if I absolutely hate it, I'll just have to tell Lester that I can't do it. Thanks, Jill. I knew you'd give me good advice."

"Don't mention it. My pleasure."

"In fact," Aunt Lucy said. "I know what I could do, if it's okay with you?"

"What's that?"

"Why don't I move in with you for a little while, and see how I like it. You could be my guide to the human world, and we'd be company for one another."

"You mean move into my flat?"

"Yeah, that would be great, wouldn't it?"

"Err — yeah. Great."

Why didn't I keep my big mouth shut? If Aunt Lucy moved in with me, it would be a disaster. Don't get me wrong, I loved her to bits. She was like a mother to me, and I'd do anything for her. Well, *almost* anything. But I really didn't want her *to live* with me. How was I meant to have any kind of love life if she moved in? I know I didn't actually *have* much of a love life, but I lived in hope. Can you imagine if I invited Jack back to the flat, and Aunt Lucy greeted him at the door? What a passion killer that would be.

***

While walking to Cuppy C, I was still trying to get my head around the idea of Aunt Lucy moving in with me. What a nightmare!

When I reached the top of the road, I spotted a crowd of people on the opposite side of the street from Cuppy C. As I drew closer, I realised the crowd was outside Best

Cakes. Were they having some kind of promotion?

Then, I noticed the twins. They were staring out of the window of Cuppy C. I expected them to be annoyed because Miles Best's shop was doing so well, but in fact both Amber and Pearl were laughing their heads off.

I was intrigued. What could be happening in Best Cakes to draw such a crowd? I crossed the road to take a closer look. The crowd outside was getting bigger by the minute, and it took me some time to fight my way through to the front. When I eventually made it, I could see what all the commotion was about. Every seat in the tea room at Best Cakes was taken, and the cake shop was also full. The strange thing was, every one of the customers in the shop was dressed as a clown. It was like my worst nightmare. I hated clowns; I'd always hated clowns. They're evil. I'd never seen so many of them in one place.

The clowns seemed to be in full flow: hitting one another in the face with custard pies, spraying water from plastic flowers, and dropping cups and saucers all over the floor. They were making a terrible mess and one heck of a racket. No wonder the twins were laughing.

A thought suddenly struck me: were the twins behind this?

I fought my way back out through the crowd, and hurried over the road to Cuppy C.

"What's Miles clowning around at?" Pearl dissolved into laughter.

"You two did this, didn't you?"

"Who? Us?" Amber feigned innocence.

"Why did you do it?"

"Have you forgotten what those two did to us?"

"You mean the rats?"

"Yes. Miles infested us with rats, so we've given him an infestation of another kind — of clowns."

"But how on earth did you organise it?"

"Have you heard of crowdfunding?" Amber wiped a tear from her eye.

"Err — yeah?"

"Well this is crowd *funning*. You can hire a crowd of whatever you want: clowns, knitters or even dentists."

"Who on earth would want to hire a crowd of dentists?"

"If the price list is anything to go by —" Pearl had just about managed to compose herself. "Not many people."

"We could have had the dentists for half the cost of the clowns," Amber said. "But we figured it was worth paying extra for the clowns. I don't think Miles will try another stunt on us in a hurry."

Chapter 19

It was ages now since Jack Maxwell had been suspended. It was time I gave him a call.

"Jack, it's Jill."

"Hi. Sorry I haven't been in touch." He sounded low.

"That's okay. I thought I should check what's happening with your suspension."

"Nothing much. Like I told you, the cogs move very slowly."

"There's *slowly* and there's *seized up*. Have you heard back from Internal Affairs?"

"Only to say the enquiry is on-going."

"On-going? What does that mean? It sounds like they need a fire under them."

"That's not how it works. It'll get sorted."

"Before or after you've retired? Why won't you let me see what I can find out?"

"No! I've told you. Keep out of this. It will only make things worse."

"Okay."

"Promise?"

"Yes, I promise."

And, as everyone knows, a successful relationship is based upon honesty and trust. Everyone apart from me, apparently.

I'd called the police station numerous times, and asked for Tom Hawk, but he was never available. I'd left messages asking him to call me back, but so far, I'd heard nothing. So, the next day, I drove to the police station in the early hours of the morning, parked across the road, and waited for him to arrive. Sure enough, just before a quarter to eight, Tom's car pulled up at the barrier. I hurried across the road, and knocked on the side window. It took him a moment to realise who I was, but then he wound the window down.

"Jill? What are you doing here? Is Jack all right?"

"If you call being suspended for weeks on end with no feedback, '*all right*', then yes, I guess he's all right. Look, Tom, what's happening? Why is the investigation taking so long?"

"It's just how these things work."

"There must be a reason why someone planted that money in his car. My guess is it's related to a case he was working on."

"I can't talk about that, and Jack wouldn't thank me for discussing his suspension with you. I'm sorry, but you're going to have to leave it alone. Internal Affairs will sort it out."

"But Tom—"

The barrier raised, and he drove through.

If Tom Hawk thought he was going to brush me off that easily, he had another think coming. I cast the 'invisible' spell, ducked under the barrier, and waited for him to get out of his car. Then, I followed him into the station. He was working out of Jack Maxwell's office.

I was sure that the information I needed would be on the computer, but to access it I was going to need the password. I stood directly behind the chair, and waited for Tom to sit down. When he did, he immediately pushed the chair backwards, and almost squashed me against the wall.

I watched closely as he entered the password—I would have to memorise every keystroke. Fortunately for me, it was laughably short and simple: HAWKEYE.

Even though I had the password, I daren't risk using the computer even when Tom stepped out of the office. There was a constant stream of people walking along the corridor outside; they would have noticed if the mouse suddenly started to move, and the screen switched display. I had no choice but to find somewhere to hide until late at night, by which time the police station should be much quieter.

The next time Tom left the office, I followed him through the door. A little way along the corridor, I found what was obviously a cleaner's cupboard. Once inside, I made my way to the very back—behind some steel shelving—where I sat down and waited. It would be a very long, boring day, but I had no choice but to wait it out.

The last time I'd checked my watch, it was eight p.m. I decided to wait until eleven, and then risk going back to Jack's office.

At least, that was the plan.

The next thing I knew, I woke up. How long had I been asleep? It was two in the morning. Great! I felt like death warmed up. I was cold, hungry, and I had no feeling in my right leg.

I listened at the door to see if I could hear anyone. It was silent. There would still be a few people around—the front desk would definitely still be manned. But I was banking on the offices being much quieter.

I made myself invisible again, and then sneaked out of

the cupboard, and down the corridor to Jack's office. Once at the computer, I waited for a couple of minutes to make sure that I couldn't hear anyone. After I'd logged in, it didn't take long to find a list of all the cases Jack had been working on the day before he was suspended.

I went through each case in turn. They had all been reassigned except for one entitled, 'Beele Casino'. That one had been closed on the day after Jack had been suspended. I was curious, so I clicked to open the file. The case had been ongoing for over a year; long before Jack Maxwell had arrived in Washbridge. So, why had it been closed so suddenly? I read more, and discovered that the case related to a casino owned by a man called Craig Beele. The notes in the file suggested that the police thought it was a front for a money laundering operation, which was being used by a number of gangs in the area.

Something didn't smell right about this. Why would a long-running case like that have been closed so suddenly? It warranted further investigation.

***

The twins were behind the counter in Cuppy C; they both had long faces.

"What's up with you two?"

"Look," Pearl pointed across the road.

Best Cakes was absolutely packed; both the tea room and cake shop were full. This time with regular customers — not clowns. I'd never seen it so busy.

"What's going on over there? Are they having a sale or something?"

"No," Amber said. "It's all the publicity they've had."

"What publicity?"

"The clown infestation. All the papers covered it. It was on the front page of the Candle."

"Oh dear." I laughed. "That kind of backfired, didn't it?"

"I warned Amber it was a stupid idea," Pearl said.

"It was *your* idea," Amber spat back.

"No it wasn't."

"Yes it was."

"No it wasn't."

"Was too."

That was my cue to leave.

Barry was doing my head in.

"Please, Jill. Please. Please, Jill. Can I go and see Babs? Please can I see Babs? She's my girlfriend."

"Be quiet, Barry. I don't know if Babs is in today."

"Can you find out? I want to see Babs. She's my girlfriend."

"Wait there." I left him upstairs while I called Dorothy. I got through first time, and she confirmed that Babs would be at her mother's house.

"Do you think your mum would mind if I went over there with Barry, and took them both out for a walk?"

"I'm sure she'd be delighted. Mum isn't as fit as she used to be, so she struggles sometimes with taking Babs for a walk. I'll give her a call, if you like, and let her know that you're coming over. When were you thinking of going?"

"Right now, if that's okay. Barry won't stop pestering me until we do."

"Okay, I'll give you her address, and let her know

you're on your way over."

Fortunately, Dorothy's mum, Dolly, lived quite close to the park where I usually walked Barry. He was so excited that I was worried he might knock Dolly over, so I tied his lead to her gate while I went to collect Babs.

"You must be Jill." Dolly was a plump, elderly lady with a round face and a pleasant smile.

"Yes. Did Dorothy tell you I was coming?"

"She did. She said you wanted to take Babs for a walk."

"That's right. If it's okay with you?"

"Yes, of course. My old legs aren't what they used to be, so I'm only able to take her around the block. If you can take her for a proper walk in the park, that would be wonderful. Dorothy said that you've got a dog too."

"Yeah, Barry. He's over there—look." I pointed to the gate.

"And these two get on well, do they?"

"They do. Barry thinks Babs is his girlfriend."

"That's nice, dear. There you go." She handed me Babs' lead.

Babs was perhaps a little less excited to see Barry than he was to see her, but they both made a fuss of one another.

Barry was much better behaved when we were with Babs than when it was just the two of us. Normally, when he and I went to the park, he would strain at the lead as soon as we got through the gates. With Babs, he was quite happy to walk beside me because she did the same.

I found a bench, and let them off their leads. They went charging around the grassed area, chasing one another around and around. They played together really nicely.

And surprisingly, they stayed where I could see them. Normally Barry would run off, and it could take me anything up to half an hour to find him again.

When it was eventually time for us to leave, I called them, and they both came straight away. That was definitely not something Barry would normally do.

I took Babs back to Dolly's house, and handed her the lead.

"Why don't you come in for a cup of tea, dear?"

"If you're sure? Barry can be rather excitable."

"He'll be fine. Come on in."

Amazingly, Babs and Barry settled down together, and began to snooze next to the fire. They'd obviously worn each other out.

"I'd like to give you something as a thank you," Dolly said.

"There's no need. You've done me a favour letting me take Babs out with us. It made the walk a much pleasanter experience."

"Still, I really would like to do something. Would you allow me to paint your portrait?"

That took me totally by surprise.

"Portrait?"

"Yes. I'm something of an artist. Didn't Dorothy tell you?"

"No. She never mentioned it. That would be very nice." I quite liked the idea of having my portrait hanging on the wall in my flat. "When did you have in mind?"

"Right now, if you like."

"Do you have time?"

"Yes, of course. Come through to my studio. It's in the back."

There were easels, paint brushes, and paints everywhere. Strangely, though, I couldn't see any completed works.

"Take a seat in the corner on that wooden chair, and we'll get started."

"How would you like me to sit?"

"Just pose naturally, dear. Perhaps looking into the distance."

I stared out through the window, and Dolly began to paint. I wondered how long it would take. I assumed that portraits could take several days, if not weeks to complete.

After an hour, I was beginning to feel a bit stiff.

"Is it all right if I just stretch my legs for a few minutes, Dolly?"

"Yes, of course, dear. I'm almost finished anyway."

Huh? After only an hour?

"I'd like you to have this as a gift."

She lifted the portrait off the easel and presented it to me.

Was this a joke? I looked at Dolly to see if she was laughing, but she seemed perfectly serious. The picture was of some kind of matchstick woman. It was the sort of thing that Lizzie would have drawn. In fact, she would have made a better job of it.

"Thank you." I didn't know what else to say.

"It's one of my better works, I think."

Once back at Cuppy C, Barry went straight upstairs to his bed, and was fast asleep in minutes. I unwrapped the portrait, and took another look—just to make sure it was as bad as I thought it was.

And then my phone rang.

"Jill?"

"Hi, Dorothy."

"Did you go to see Mum?"

"Yes. I took Barry and Babs for a walk. They played very nicely together."

"That's great. Any time you feel like doing it again, I'm sure Mum will be only too pleased."

"I will." I hesitated. "There is just one thing though, Dorothy."

"Yes?"

"Your mum offered to do my portrait while I was there."

"Oh, no." Dorothy laughed. "You didn't let her, did you?"

"Yeah."

"Was it terrible?"

"Well—"

"You can tell me, Jill. I've seen her paintings."

"It wasn't particularly good. It looked like a child had done it."

"Yeah. She's always doing portraits for people, and they're always terrible. But no one has the heart to tell her. You won't say anything, will you?"

"No. Of course not."

"Thanks. By the way, Jill, did you have a chance to look into that *other thing*?"

"Other thing?"

"The human blood thing?"

"Oh, *that* other thing." It had completely slipped my mind. "I'm still on it. I'll get back to you as soon as I can."

"Thanks, Jill, you're a life-saver."

I really should get one of those fancy to-do apps. My

memory wasn't as good as—err—something or other.

Chapter 20

I didn't want to run the risk of forgetting about Dorothy's *little problem* again, so I contacted Alan, Pearl's fiancé, and asked if I could have a few words in private. He was understandably intrigued, but readily agreed.

When I told him about the issue Dorothy had been struggling with since she moved to Washbridge, he didn't seem at all surprised. Apparently it was quite a common problem. Unlike most other sups who transitioned to the human world with relative ease, vampires often found it quite a struggle. For a vampire who had lived for twenty years or more in the sup world, and who had been used to only synthetic blood, suddenly being surrounded by humans could prove to be very difficult. That's why more vampires failed to integrate into the human world than any of the other sups.

None of this was very encouraging for Dorothy.

Alan was able to give me one piece of advice though. He had friends who'd had similar problems when they'd moved to the human world. They'd visited a support group called 'No Fangs'. In every case, the support group had helped them to get through that initial, difficult period. Before he left, Alan gave me the name of a contact at the local Washbridge branch of No Fangs.

I called them, and spoke to a man called Declan De Stein. He was quite surprised to be contacted by a witch. Most of his calls, understandably, came from vampires. I explained the situation: that I had a friend, a vampire, who was struggling to resist human blood. I told him that before I recommended his support group, I wondered if I might sit in on a session. He was obviously a little surprised by my request, but said he could see no reason why I shouldn't attend as an observer. Their next meeting was that same night, so I said I'd see him there later.

***

I'd changed into my black suit because I needed to look the part for my visit to Beele Casino. It was mid-morning when I arrived there. As I'd expected, the doors were locked. A sign in the window showed the opening hours were midday to four a.m. every day.

I pressed the button on the intercom, and a few seconds later a man's voice answered.

"We're closed."

"D.I. Lane. Washbridge Police. Open the door, please."

"What do you want?"

"I'm here to see Craig Beele."

"Hold on."

The line went silent, but then a few minutes later, a man built like a tank opened the door. The badge on his breast pocket read 'Security'.

"Follow me." He growled.

The casino was deserted except for a few cleaning staff. The man-tank led me to an office at the back of the building. Behind the desk was a man with black, slicked-back hair; he was wearing a gold ring, which was shaped like a kangaroo. If you were to check the word 'slime' in the dictionary, you'd probably find a picture of this man.

"Craig Beele?" I said, in my best police officer voice.

"What do you want?"

"As Jack Maxwell is on gardening leave, I've been assigned to your case."

"My case? There is no case. It's been closed. You'd better go back and check your records."

"No need. This case is very much alive, and I have a few questions I'd like to ask you."

"There's obviously been a mistake. I was told officially that all investigations into myself and the casino have now ended."

"Told officially by who?"

His face flushed red with anger. "I don't have to answer your questions."

"Who told you the case was closed?" I pressed.

"I'm not talking to you or any other police officer unless my solicitor is present."

"In that case, I must ask you and your solicitor to report to the station later today. Ask for D.I. Lane."

"We'll see about that."

"I'll expect you later."

He mumbled something under his breath, and then gestured for the security man to escort me out. Once outside, I quickly made my way around the back of the casino. I'd mapped out the building in my mind, so it was relatively easy to position myself directly outside Beele's office.

It didn't surprise me to discover that he was already on the phone, and courtesy of the 'listen' spell, I was able to hear every word he said.

"What's going on?" he yelled down the phone. "I thought you'd sorted this out?"

I could hear his footsteps as he paced back and forth across the room.

"You can't have, can you? I just had a visit from some stuck-up little cow of a copper."

Stuck-up little cow? What a charmer.

"Just now. I can't remember—D.I. Pain or Lane or something."

Something crashed against the wall. He was throwing things about now. Perhaps I'd upset him?

"You'd better get your backside down here, and sharpish. I'm paying you enough. I don't expect to have to do your work for you. I don't care! Get over here now!"

With that, Beele ended the call. That had been exactly the response I'd hoped for.

The pillars of the building opposite provided ample cover while I waited. Fifteen minutes later, a car pulled up outside the casino.

Yes! Just as I'd expected.

I made myself invisible, and followed the man into the casino. He made a beeline for Beele's office. Once there, I switched on the digital recorder which was in my pocket.

***

"Jill? I wasn't expecting to see you." I'd turned up at Jack's flat unannounced.

"Nice joggers, Jack." I couldn't hide my grin.

Blaze would have approved of Maxwell's luminous green jogging bottoms.

"They were a present from my auntie."

"Doesn't she like you?"

"Did you come here just to insult my clothes or was there another reason?"

"If you ask me in, I might tell you."

"Sorry." He stepped aside. "Come in. Do you want a drink?"

"Not right now. I need to talk to you about your suspension."

His demeanour changed immediately. "I've told you already. I don't want you getting involved. Internal Affairs will—"

"Yeah, yeah, I know. Internal Affairs will sort it out."

"I mean it, Jill. Keep out of it."

"Whoops! Too late, I'm afraid."

"What have you done now?"

"Sit down, and I'll tell you."

"I don't want to sit down. I want to know what you've been up to."

"Sit down, please."

"I'm okay standing."

"You are the most exasperating man!"

"Coming from you, that's pretty rich. Now, will you tell me what you've done?"

"Listen to this."

I took the digital recorder out of my pocket and pressed 'play'.

"What's going on?"

"That's Craig Beele." Maxwell stared at the recorder.

"What did you say her name was?"

"That's Tom. What is this, Jill?"

"Just listen. I'll answer your questions afterwards.

"I told you. She said her name was D.I. Pain or Lane."

"We don't have a D.I. Pain or Lane."

"Well, I didn't dream her up. She was standing right where you are less than thirty minutes ago."

"What did she say?"

"That she wanted to ask me questions about my case. My case! You told me that it had been closed."

"It has. I closed it as soon as I got Maxwell thrown off the job."

"Well, it looks like someone has re-opened it."

"That's impossible. I'd know."

"What are you going to do about it? She wants me down at the station later today with my solicitor."

"Don't do anything. Not until I find out what's going on."

"You'd better do that, and fast. I didn't pay you all that money to have to deal with this."

"I'll get it sorted."

"Phone me when you have."

"I can't believe it." Maxwell said. "Tom? Why would he do this to me?"

"He's screwed you over right and proper. I don't need two guesses who planted the cash in your car."

"He and I are meant to be friends."

"You know what they say. With friends like him —"

"How did you get this?"

"I have my methods."

"I told you to stay out of it." He pulled me close. "Thanks for ignoring me." Then he planted a kiss on my lips. I was so shocked that I hardly had time to respond before he'd pulled away.

"I have to go," he said.

"Where?"

"It's time I had a few words with Internal Affairs." He grabbed the digital recorder. "And with Tom Hawk."

"One word of advice, if I may?" I shouted after him.

"What's that?"

"Change out of those joggers first."

***

With a bit of luck, Jack would be back at his desk soon. That was one less thing for me to worry about. But he hadn't been the only man playing on my mind.

Ever since I'd bumped into my father at the Fleur Hotel, I hadn't been able to get him out of my head. Before that day, it had been quite easy for me to push him to the back of my mind; he hadn't seemed real. But now I'd actually met him, it was much more difficult. In the end, I succumbed to what was probably no more than curiosity, and called the number on the card that he'd given me. He sounded both surprised and pleased to hear from me. We arranged to meet in the late afternoon of the following day in a small coffee shop called Caffeine Cellar.

***

The No Fangs meeting was being held in a disused chapel, in a seedy area of Washbridge. Declan met me at the door, and said he'd informed the other members of the group that I'd be attending the meeting. No-one had any objections provided I was there merely to observe, and didn't try to participate. I readily agreed.

"It's all very informal." He led me through to what was obviously the main room. It was very cold inside, and quite dark too. There were eight or nine vampires, a mix of men and women, sitting in a circle. As I walked in, I could feel their eyes on me.

"Take a seat over there, Jill."

After I joined them in the circle, Declan took his seat. "Okay everyone, before we start today's meeting, this is Jill Gooder who I told you about earlier."

They all glanced at me, and for some reason, I suddenly felt very uneasy.

"We don't get many other kinds of sups in here, but Jill asked if she could check out what we do, and report back to a vampire friend of hers who's having the usual struggles. So please make her welcome."

A couple of them said 'hi', and smiled at me. As they did, I could see their fangs. That was quite unusual; vampires usually managed to hide their fangs in public. I was feeling more and more uncomfortable.

"Okay. Let's kick things off," Declan said. "Marcia, how have things been with you this week?"

"Not so good really, Declan. I was doing okay, but then I had to take the bus because my car was being serviced. I sat next to this young human. It was terrible. His blood—I could almost taste it! All I could think of was sinking my fangs into his neck."

"It's okay, Marcia, we've all been there. Hopefully, you managed to resist?"

"I did, Declan. I had a bottle of synthetic in my pocket, so I took a quick drink of that. He probably thought it was blackcurrant juice. I got off the bus a couple of stops early; the walk helped to clear my head."

"You did very well, Marcia. Didn't she, everyone?"

They all nodded and smiled in approval, but then all eyes were back on me again. And now *everyone's* fangs were showing. What was going on? I'd assumed they were only interested in human blood, but I had a horrible feeling that they no longer saw me as an observer, more as a meal.

"Okay, Declan, thanks for letting me sit in." I stood up. "I think I've seen enough."

"But we've only just started."

"Yeah, no, it's fine. It seems like you're doing an excellent job. I'll be happy to recommend that my friend attends. Can she come next week?"

"Yes, of course. Tell her to pop in."

"Okay." I began to back slowly towards the door. I half expected one of them to break ranks, and chase after me.

Phew! I was glad to get out of there. I'd never had the slightest concern about vampires before, but then I'd never been alone in a room full of them.

I called Dorothy.

"About your little problem."

"Did you come up with anything?" I could hear the hope in her voice.

"Yeah. There's a group which meets once a week in Washbridge called No Fangs."

"Seriously?"

"Terrible name, I know. It's for vampires like you who are struggling to resist the temptation of human blood."

"And do you think it will help?"

"I think so. My cousin's fiancé says it helped several of his friends."

"I don't suppose you'd come with me for my first visit, would you?"

"Sorry. I don't think that would be a good idea. You'll be okay though. I'll text you the address. The next meeting is a week today. Just ask for Declan."

"Okay, Jill. That's another one I owe you."

Chapter 21

I'd overslept, but so what? I could go in late if I wanted. I was eating cornflakes when the phone rang. It was Kathy.

"Jill, have you seen The Bugle?"

"No. I'm still at the flat. I overslept. Why?"

"They've run an article on Ever."

Dougal Bugle had told me that he planned to run an exposé on Ever A Wool Moment. Things were difficult enough with the new competition from Best Wool. The last thing Grandma needed was more bad news.

"Oh dear. Is Grandma up in arms about it?"

"No. Quite the opposite. She's really quite pleased."

"Very funny."

"I'm serious. She thinks it's great."

"How come?"

"Hold on—she's calling me. Got to dash, sorry. Buy a copy, and take a look for yourself."

"Kathy?" She was gone.

I was intrigued, so I threw on some clothes, and popped over the road to the newsagent. Jasper James was wearing a yellow fedora, and was engrossed in a magazine.

I coughed to get his attention.

"Sorry, Jill. I didn't notice you there."

"What's that you're reading?"

"Fedora Weekly."

I should have known.

He checked his watch. "You're usually in earlier than this. Are you on holiday?"

"No. Just running a little late—I overslept."

"I have just the magazine for you: 'Alarm Clock

Enthusiast'."

I smiled. Everyone's a comedian.

Then, to my amazement, he produced said magazine from the shelf.

"See. Everything you could ever want to know about alarm clocks. Would you like a copy?"

Back at my flat, I laid The Bugle on the kitchen table. There was nothing about Ever on the front page; that was a relief. Perhaps Grandma had somehow persuaded Dougal to bury the article in the inside pages. I flicked through, page after page, but there was no sign of it. Then, I realised that the centre pages were actually a pull-out feature.

What? Unbelievable!

The whole pull-out was dedicated to Ever A Wool Moment. It covered: Everlasting Wool, One-Size Knitting Needles and Ever membership. There was even a write-up on the tea room, complete with photographs. The article was very upbeat with glowing reports on all aspects of the business. The whole thing was as good as a giant advert for Ever A Wool Moment.

What had happened to the article Dougal had told me he intended to print? Grandma must have used magic; nothing else could account for such a complete turnaround. Somehow, she'd once again come out smelling of roses.

***

Madeline dropped by at lunch time; she was dressed in her librarian outfit. It was almost like knowing two different people — the contrast between her two personas: Madeline and Mad, was so pronounced.

"Hey, Mad. How goes the librarian life?"

"Boring as ever. Are you sure you don't need someone to work with you? I could see myself as a private investigator."

"I can barely find enough work to keep myself afloat, I'm afraid. Besides, your dress sense is hardly suited to the P.I. life."

"You mean this outfit?"

"No. I meant your after work gear. It can be a bit outrageous."

"Only a bit? I must be mellowing." She grinned.

"So, to what do I owe this pleasure?"

"It's a bit awkward, really. I've been approached by your grandmother."

"What did *she* want?"

"She asked if I'd like to open a franchise of Ever A Wool Moment in Ghost Town."

"Do ghosts knit?"

"Apparently, they do. According to your grandmother, research has shown that per head of population, ghosts knit more than humans."

"You learn something new every day. Does that apply to sups too? If so, I'm surprised she hasn't opened a branch in Candlefield."

"I wondered about that myself, but I didn't like to ask her."

"Maybe she feels it would undermine her credibility as a witch? Grandma is one of the most powerful witches in Candlefield. Opening a wool shop might detract from that image. How do you feel about taking on the franchise?

You're always saying that you're bored with being a librarian."

"It's a non-starter. If I was to take her up on her offer, I'd have to quit my job as a Ghost Hunter. If nothing else, ghost hunting is a secure, well-paid job, so it would be a big risk for me to give it up. And anyway, can you see me working in a wool shop?"

"No, but then I couldn't see you working in a library either."

"I'd be useless. I know about as much about wool as you do."

"You'd be surprised how much I know about wool these days. What with Mrs V and Grandma, I'm becoming quite the expert."

"I'm a bit worried about how your grandmother's going to take it when I say no. I get the impression she's not used to people saying no to her."

"You're right there. Look, if you like, I'll tell her that you don't want to do it."

"You will?"

"Yeah, why not? I mean, she's already got it in for me."

***

I arrived ten minutes ahead of time for my meeting with my father. I ordered a latte, but couldn't face anything to eat even though they had some delicious looking muffins. I had no appetite; my stomach was churning.

He arrived on the dot, and without even bothering to order a drink, came over and joined me at my table.

"Thanks for seeing me, Jill."

"I don't have long. I have to meet someone in fifteen

minutes. Just say whatever it is you want to say to me."

"I'd like to start by explaining why I wasn't in your life when you were growing up."

"No explanation necessary. You walked out. Seems pretty straightforward to me."

"I had no idea Darlene was pregnant when I left."

"Would it have made a difference if you had known?"

He hesitated. "Probably not. Things had gone very badly for me in a short space of time. I'd made some very bad decisions that had come back to haunt me. I had to put some distance between myself and the ones I loved — to protect them."

"Oh, I see. So it was a purely unselfish act on your part?"

"No. I would never claim that. It was my selfishness that got me into that situation in the first place, but I left to protect Darlene."

"Did you *ever* love my mother?"

He looked surprised by the question. "Of course I did." He glanced down at the table. "I still do."

His answer threw me for a moment. "Why come back now?"

"To warn you of the danger you are in. During my exile, I met many people. Some of them good, but a lot of them bad. But none as evil as TDO."

"What exactly do you know about TDO?"

"Too much."

"Do you know who he is and where he is?"

"It'll be safer for you if I don't answer those questions."

"Don't give me that. Either you know him or you don't."

"I can't tell you any more than I already have."

"Are you TDO?" I challenged him.

"Me?" He seemed stunned by the question.

"You never did explain why you were at the Fleur Hotel."

"I was looking for you."

"So you said."

"It's true. I had to warn you."

"About what?"

"I've heard that TDO has declared you must be eliminated soon."

"Heard? Heard from who?"

"I'd rather—"

"You'd rather not say—I get it. So what if he says I have to be eliminated? What's new? He's been trying to kill me ever since I discovered I was a witch."

"Time's running out for him."

"What do you mean?"

"He's seen how rapidly you've progressed through the levels. It's totally unprecedented. If he doesn't eliminate you soon, it'll be too late. You'll be too powerful."

"You seem to know an awful lot about TDO. Why would I trust anything you say?"

"Because despite what you may think, I love you."

"Too little, too late." I stood up. "You've had your say, now. I never want to see or hear from you again."

***

After my brief meeting with my father, I didn't really want to go straight home. I knew if I did, I'd spend all evening brooding about what he'd said. I wanted to forget all about him in the same way he'd once forgotten about me.

I called Kathy, and she said I could pop over to her house.

"How's Peter's business doing?"

"It's coming along quite nicely actually." Kathy had bought a new kettle, but had not yet figured out how to get it working. "He's picking up new customers every week. He did a leafleting campaign around the local neighbourhood a while back, and he landed some new business from that. In fact, he's working at a house just down the road right now."

"Do you need a hand with that?"

"No. It's only a stupid kettle. How difficult can it be?"

"You've been at it for ten minutes."

"They make everything way too complicated nowadays. Look at all these buttons. It's only a kettle. Why does it need all of these?"

"I think I see the problem."

"Come on then, Miss Smartypants. Let's see you work it out."

I walked over to the socket on the wall, and clicked the switch to the 'On' position.

"That should do it."

Kathy sighed. "Do you think that was my first senior moment?"

Just then, the door opened, and in walked Peter, looking sweaty and tired, but with a huge smile on his face.

"What are you doing here?" Kathy said. "You should be working — earning money for me to spend on clothes."

"I needed a break. I couldn't see the point of sitting out there with a flask when I was only two minutes from home. I thought I'd pop back for a cup of tea, and one of your finest muffins."

"You're in luck. Jill just showed me how to use the new kettle."

"How's it going, Peter?" I said.

"Not bad at all. I've been working at an old guy's house down the road—a Mr Durham. Nice chap, but crazy as a box of frogs. You'll never guess what he was telling me this morning, Kathy."

"Has he seen more aliens?"

"No, not aliens this time. Apparently he saw a zombie in his backyard last week."

"A zombie?" Kathy laughed. "Wow, that old guy really does have an active imagination."

"Yeah, and that's not all. According to Mr Durham, a woman turned up and shot the zombie in the head. Then it just disintegrated."

Kathy and Peter both laughed.

"Yeah, that old guy sounds really crazy," I said.

There was a knock on the door.

"I'll get it." Kathy headed out of the kitchen.

Moments later, she returned, accompanied by an old man. "Pete, it's Mr Durham."

The old man walked unsteadily into the room. "You left before I could pay you."

"You needn't have come over, Mr Durham. I haven't finished up yet."

"I like to pay my debts on time." He glanced over at me, and did a double-take. "It's her!"

"That's my sister," Kathy said. "That's Jill."

"She's the one!"

Peter and Kathy both stared at him.

"She's the zombie killer!"

When Kathy had eventually managed to calm Mr Durham down, Peter said he'd walk him back to his house. After they'd left, I jumped in first.

"You've got some crazy neighbours."

"Maybe." Kathy gave me a doubtful look.

"What do you mean, *maybe*? Didn't you hear what he just said? He said there was a zombie in his backyard."

"He also said you were the one who destroyed it. Where exactly did you go the other night when you said you had cramp?"

I raised my hands in mock surrender. "Gee. You got me. I'm actually a zombie hunter. That's why I was hiding in the bus shelter. I was waiting for a zombie to turn up."

Kathy stared at me for the longest moment, and then dissolved into laughter. "I think I'm cracking up. It must be all the drumming that Mikey does."

"Still," I said. "It would be a pretty cool job—being a zombie hunter."

Phew! Another bullet dodged.

***

Just the man I wanted to see.

"Luther!" I called after him.

"Hi, Jill."

"I'm glad I caught up with you."

"It's not every day I have women chasing after me."

I found that hard to believe.

"You know Betty Longbottom, don't you?"

"Betty? Yes, we've spoken a few times, but never for

more than a few minutes."

"Did you know she was a tax inspector?"

"I think she did mention it."

"Well, she paid me a visit the other day, and more or less accused me of paying Mrs V off-the-books."

"Isn't that your P.A? The knitter?"

"That's her."

"I thought you didn't pay her at all?"

"I don't, but Betty thinks otherwise. Anyway, she insists on seeing my accountant."

"I see. Well, don't worry. I'll put her straight."

"Would you call on her to arrange a meeting between the two of you?"

"Of course. No problem. I'm sure I'll be able to answer all of her questions to her satisfaction."

"That's exactly what I told her. I said if anyone can satisfy her, it would be you."

"I'll let you know how I get on."

"Thanks."

Poor Luther. He had no idea what he'd let himself in for.

Snigger.

Chapter 22

The temperature in my office dropped, and I knew either my mother or the colonel was about to appear. Winky hissed; he hated it when ghosts were around.

"Morning, Jill." The colonel beamed.

"Morning, Jill." Priscilla was by his side. They were arm in arm. Love's young dream.

"Hello you two. I see you're getting on famously."

They smiled at each other, and for a moment were lost in one another's eyes. How very—sickening—I mean sweet.

"Thanks for the heads up about our friend, Battery, Colonel. It's all sorted now."

"My pleasure, Jill. Only too happy to help. I hate to think of you coming to any harm because of an idiot like that. What happened to him, anyway?"

"I have a friend who's a parahuman. By day she's a librarian, but by night she's a Ghost Hunter."

"Really?" Priscilla said. "That sounds very exciting."

"She apprehended Battery; his haunting days have been well and truly curtailed. I definitely owe you one."

"Funny you should say that, Jill." The colonel grinned. "We were wondering if you might be able to do us a small favour." He looked at Priscilla, who giggled. She giggled a lot. She and the twins would have got on famously.

"I will if I can." What had I let myself in for now?

"The thing is, although we have our own places in Ghost Town, we'd both rather like to have somewhere in the human world where we could spend some time."

"I thought you already had somewhere: my office."

"We do pop in here rather often, don't we?" He

laughed. "We were actually thinking of somewhere a little more permanent—you know, a proper home. Somewhere we could haunt on a permanent basis."

"Did you have anywhere in mind?"

"I do actually. I know exactly the place."

"Are you talking about your old house?"

"Got it in one. I spent a lot of time and money on that house. It seems a pity to let someone else get all the benefit."

"Who owns it now?"

"That's why we've come to see you. As per my Will, it was sold, and the proceeds split between the dog charity, Mrs Burnbridge and Peter. But I don't actually know who bought the old place. So we were wondering if maybe you could take a run up there sometime to find out who the new owners are. And to see if they're the sort of people who wouldn't be too freaked out by the idea of ghosts sharing their home."

"No problem. I'll take a drive over there later today."

"Thanks, Jill. You're a diamond."

Diamond? Don't remind me.

"Come on, Cilla." The colonel took her arm. "We'd better get going. I've booked a table for lunch. Bye, Jill."

***

It felt strange to be back at the colonel's house knowing that he no longer lived there. It was a beautiful house, and although I'd only been there a few times, I'd grown very fond of it.

Externally at least, nothing seemed to have changed. I rang the bell, but there was no answer. I tried again, and this time the door opened to reveal a man in a butler's outfit. I'd always assumed all butlers wore black suits. This man's suit was red. Or perhaps, more accurately, crimson.

"Hello, madam."

"Hi."

"You're a little late."

"I am?"

"Yes, but it's all right. Follow me."

What a stroke of luck. He obviously thought I was someone else. If I could just get to speak with the new owners, I could try to get a feel for if they'd be open to the idea of ghostly visitors.

Halfway across the hall, the butler stopped and pointed to the room on the right.

"That's the green room, madam. You can get undressed in there."

"I'm sorry?"

"The green room. You can get undressed in there."

"Why would I want to get undressed?"

He looked puzzled. "Aren't you here for the open day?"

"Err—no. I was hoping to speak to the owner of this property."

"Mr Nolan?"

"I guess so. Is that possible?"

"I'll have to check. He's out on the terrace. Who shall I say wishes to speak to him?"

"Jill Gooder. I'm a good friend of Colonel Briggs who used to own this house."

"Very well. Would you wait there for a moment?"

"Certainly."

The interior of the house hadn't changed dramatically. There were a few new paintings, but otherwise, it was practically the same as the last time I'd been there.

The crimson-clad butler returned a couple of minutes later.

"Mr Nolan will see you now. Please follow me."

We walked through the house and out through the large French doors at the rear. The sight that greeted me took my breath away. There were at least twenty people: some on sun loungers, some playing volleyball, and others playing a game of badminton. And, they were all naked! Stark naked!

The butler led me to a man sitting in a deckchair. In one hand, he had a huge cigar; in the other, he was holding an enormous glass of wine. Middle-aged, he was more than a little overweight. His grey hair was pulled back into a ponytail. He too, was stark naked.

"Hello, Mr Nolan," I said, fixing my gaze firmly on his face. "I'm Jill Gooder."

"Nice to meet you, Jill. I never met the colonel, but from all accounts, he was a good sort. Tragic what happened to him. I've been on the lookout for somewhere to base our little club for some time, so when this property came on the market, I leaped at the chance."

"Club?"

"Yes. This house is now home to Washbridge Naturist Society. Do you have an interest in naturism?"

"No. It isn't really my thing. I get goosebumps very easily."

"Pity. We're always on the lookout for new blood — that's why we're having an open day. Now, what was it you wanted to see me about?"

"I was just passing, actually. I still have a soft spot for this house, so I thought I'd call in on the off chance I'd be able to have one last look at the old place. It doesn't look like you've changed very much—other than the nakedness, obviously."

"I've made a few changes, but nothing much. The colonel had excellent taste."

"Have you seen the ghosts yet?"

He looked surprised. "Ghosts? No. I wasn't aware that there were any ghosts."

"Oh, yes. The house has been haunted for quite some time. The colonel often used to see them."

"How very interesting. I do hope they turn up. I like all things supernatural."

"Really? Well, I have a hunch that you may be seeing them very soon."

"Are you sure I can't interest you in our club? The human body is nothing to be ashamed of, you know."

"Err—no. Thanks anyway." I glanced at my watch. "Gosh, is that the time. I'd better get going. I have an appointment with my—err—cat."

"With your cat?"

"I meant cat groomer. His fur is in a bit of a mess. The cat's that is—not the groomer's. Better dash. Thanks for seeing me."

***

I was helping Pearl out in Cuppy C. Amber was upstairs. She'd been complaining of toothache for a couple of hours; the poor mite had looked in agony.

I didn't notice Maxine Jewell come in until she appeared in front of me at the counter.

"Hello, Maxine." I treated her to my falsest smile. "What can I get for you today?"

"I don't want anything to drink. I'm here to see you."

"My lucky day, then."

"Always got a smart word to say, haven't you, Gooder?"

"I do my best. What is it you want, Maxine?"

"I'd like you to come down to the police station with me."

"I don't think so, but thanks for the invite."

"It's not an invitation; it's an order."

"What have I done now?"

"Inspector Lyndon, my boss, would like a word with you."

"What about?"

"Just come with me. He'll explain when we get down there."

I could have argued, but it wasn't as though I was really needed in Cuppy C; it was deadly quiet. And, I had to admit, I was curious why Maxine's boss wanted to see me.

Inspector Lyndon was a tall, thin man with a long pointed nose; he greeted me with a warm smile, and a friendly handshake. All very disconcerting.

"So you're the famous Jill Gooder. I've heard and read a lot about you."

"All bad, I assume?"

"No, far from it."

"Why did you want to see me, Inspector?"

"I'd actually like your help; if you're prepared to assist

us."

I glanced across at Maxine Jewell. I could tell that she wasn't happy about this at all, which made me even more keen to get involved.

"Gladly, Inspector. How can I help?"

"We have a rather strange situation on our hands. Over the last few weeks there have been multiple thefts on the buses which run from Washbridge to Candlefield."

"I had no idea there was public transport between the two towns."

"There's no reason you would know. As a witch, you're able to use magic to travel back and forth between the two. Wizards can too. But the other sups have to rely on more conventional means of transport. And for those who don't have a car, public transport is the only option. There are two buses each way, every day. The ones from Washbridge run at midday and midnight. The midnight bus has experienced problems on at least four occasions now. When the bus arrived in Candlefield, the passengers found that they'd been robbed of their money and other valuables."

"Who did it?"

"That's the strange thing. No one on board the bus remembers it happening. The first they knew about it was when they got to Candlefield, and realised that their money and valuables were missing."

"So you're saying they didn't see anyone do it?"

"That's precisely it. It's a mystery really. Anyway, the reason I asked you to come in is that we need someone to go undercover on that bus."

"What about your own people?"

"We need someone who is familiar with Washbridge

and Candlefield. Unfortunately, it's a condition of service that those in the police force do not visit the human world. So, you see my problem?"

"Yes. But won't the fact that I'm a witch alert the thieves?"

"No reason it should. Witches and wizards often use the buses. Not because they need to, but because they enjoy the experience."

"So you'd like me to travel on the bus, and see if I notice anything unusual?"

"Precisely that."

"Okay. I'll be happy to help."

***

When I got back to Cuppy C, Amber was back downstairs, and sitting at a table with William.

"How's the toothache?"

"Not good." She was holding her mouth. "I'm still getting a lot of pain."

"Oh, dear. When are you going to the dentist?"

"I've called him, but he can't fit me in for a couple of days. I'll just have to take painkillers until then." She turned to William. "I think I'll go back to bed, and try to get to sleep."

William gave her a gentle peck on the forehead.

After Amber had gone, I joined William at the table. "Poor Amber."

"I know. She's really suffering, poor girl. It's a pity that the dentist can't see her sooner."

"Hey, William, did you know there's a bus service between Candlefield and Washbridge?"

"Of course. Didn't you realise?"

"No. It never even occurred to me."

"It's all right for witches and wizards, but the rest of us have to travel the more conventional route. I'm okay because I've got a car now, but when I was a kid, we always used to go on the bus. Back then, they used to take the old route before they built the new road. Anyway, I'd better get back to work. Nice seeing you, Jill."

"Yeah, you too, William."

Chapter 23

I was in my office; Winky was asleep. I wasn't sure if I'd be able to contact the colonel, but I thought I'd give it a try.

"Colonel? Are you there?

There was no response, so I tried again. "Colonel? Priscilla? Are you there?"

Suddenly, I felt a slight chill, and the colonel appeared, arm in arm with Priscilla.

"You called, Jill?"

"I visited your old house as you asked."

"Has it changed much?"

"Very little in fact. The exterior of the house looks exactly the same. And inside, there are some new paintings, but other than that, it's pretty much the same old place."

"Excellent. I was worried someone might have gutted it."

"Nothing to worry about on that score."

"Did you get a feel for whether the new owner might be receptive to a haunting?"

"I did actually. He seems very open to the idea."

"That's great news, isn't it, Cilla?"

"There is one *slight* problem though, Colonel."

"What's that?"

"The man who bought the house is the head of the local naturist society, and he's using the house as a base for his club."

The colonel looked rather taken aback. "Naturists? You mean *naked people*?"

"That's right."

"Were there any naked people there when you visited?"

"Quite a few of them, including the owner himself. In fact, the only person who wasn't naked was the butler. They were playing badminton and volleyball around the back of the house."

"In the nude?"

"Yes. To tell you the truth, I was a little embarrassed."

It looked as though Priscilla was too. She was blushing.

"This has come as rather a shock." The colonel certainly looked stunned. "We'll need to give this some serious thought, won't we, Cilla?"

"I'm not sure I can live among naked people, Briggsy." Her face was the same shade as the butler's suit.

"Yes. That could be a deal-breaker. Anyway, thanks again, Jill."

***

I'd never been to Washbridge bus station before. My adoptive parents had always had a car, and I'd been able to drive from the age of seventeen, so I'd never needed to take the bus. The place was practically deserted, but then it was a quarter to midnight. I found the ticket office, but when I got to the counter, it suddenly occurred to me there might be a problem.

"Can I have a single to Candlefield, please?"

"To where?"

"Candlefield."

"Never heard of it, love, sorry."

"Right. Okay, thanks."

What was I supposed to do now? I had no idea where to catch the bus, and even if I found it, I didn't have a ticket.

I wandered around, unsure what to do, but then I spotted two werewolves.

"Excuse me?"

"Yes?"

"Do you have any idea where I can catch the bus to Candlefield?"

"Why do you need the bus? Surely you can just magic yourself there, can't you?"

"I could, but I have a thing about buses. It's kind of a hobby."

"Whatever floats your boat." He gave me a sympathetic look. "We're on our way to catch it ourselves."

I followed them to the far side of the bus station where a bus was waiting. The panel on the front read: *'Bus not in service'*.

I was beginning to think they'd played a trick on me, but then the driver opened the doors, let us on, and took our fares. It was a double decker, and I decided to sit right at the front on the upper deck. There weren't many passengers—probably half a dozen on the upper deck, and a few more on the lower deck.

We'd soon left Washbridge behind, and were in the countryside. There were no streetlights on that stretch of road, so I couldn't see much of anything through the windows. We'd been travelling for a while when my phone rang. It was Mrs V. Why on earth would she be calling at that time of night?

I was just about to press the 'Answer' button when the called dropped; I had no signal whatsoever. I glanced outside, and could see we'd stopped in a tunnel of some kind. No wonder I'd lost the call.

I'd planned to call Mrs V back as soon as we moved off,

and were out of the tunnel, but I must have nodded off because the next thing I knew, I was waking up as the bus pulled into Candlefield bus station. I was just about to make my way downstairs when a vampire, a few seats behind me, shouted, "Hey! My wallet's missing!"

Moments later, one of the werewolves who I'd seen at the bus station shouted, "Mine's gone too!"

Before long, everybody was saying the same thing. Everyone had been robbed. I checked for my purse; it had gone.

But how?

As soon as I stepped off the bus, Maxine Jewell appeared, and pulled me to one side.

"What happened, Gooder?"

"Nothing. Nothing happened. It was a very straightforward bus journey."

"Well, clearly something happened, because everybody on the bus has been robbed. What about you?"

"My purse has gone."

"Brilliant! I knew it was a waste of time getting you involved. I warned the inspector that you were useless. I'm going to ask him to take you off the case. We don't need semi-witches interfering in police business."

"Don't hold back, Maxine. Say what you really think."

"Amateurs!" And with that, she stormed off.

I was exhausted, and still felt only half-awake. And to top it off, I had a horrible taste in my mouth — like I'd just eaten an unripe banana. Yuk! I was really annoyed with myself. What kind of a private investigator was I, to fall asleep on the job?

I was still tired when I arrived at the office later that morning. And I still had that horrible banana taste in my mouth even though I'd brushed my teeth and rinsed with mouthwash. Maybe I was coming down with something.

"Mrs V, what are you doing?"

It was like déjà vu. Mrs V was on her way out, carrying a box full of her belongings: knitting needles, crochet hooks, and any number of patterns.

"I tried to call you last night, Jill, but you didn't answer your phone."

"Sorry, I was in a tunnel."

"Tunnel?"

"Long story. Never mind that. What's happened? Why have you packed your things? I thought you and I were okay?"

"We are. Of course we are. I got a telephone call late last night. G has been rushed into hospital."

"Your sister? What's wrong with her?"

"I'm not sure. Her heart, I think. I have to go down there to look after her."

Mrs V was such a selfless soul. Not everyone would have dropped everything to look after someone who'd treated them so badly.

"I'm sorry to hear that. Do you know how long you'll be gone?"

"I've no idea, but I suspect it will be some time. That's why I'm taking my knitting and crocheting. I'll need something to pass the time." She checked her watch. "I've got a taxi booked in five minutes. I'd better say goodbye."

"You'll keep me posted?"

"Of course, but you might need to get someone in because I have a feeling I may be gone for some time."

"Take care of yourself."

"Don't worry about me, dear. I'll be fine. Goodbye then."

"Goodbye, Mrs V."

Poor old Mrs V. And poor old me. What was I going to do without my P.A? I walked into my office, and had to dodge the party popper that came whizzing past my head.

"What do you think you're doing?" I yelled at Winky.

"Champagne?" He offered me a glass.

"What's the occasion?"

"What do you think? The old bag lady has left. Now you can get in a pretty young thing who adores cats." He let off another party popper.

***

I'd have to sort out Mrs V's replacement later. First, I was determined to solve the mystery of the bus robberies. I'd prove to Maxine Jewell that I was no amateur.

I magicked myself to Candlefield police station, and asked to see the inspector.

"Didn't go very well, did it, Jill?" He didn't look happy.

"No, it didn't."

"In fact, it was a spectacular failure. Maxine wants me to kick you off the case."

"Look, Inspector—I know things didn't work out last night, but I'm still willing to pursue this if you'll allow me to."

"I can give you another forty-eight hours, but that's all. Then I'll have to take you off the case. Otherwise, I'll have Maxine on my back."

"Would it be okay if I looked through your records on these robberies?"

"Of course. I'll call the records office, and have someone collect you. They'll let you see whatever you need to."

A few minutes later, a young police officer escorted me down two flights of stairs to the records office. With her help, I was able to access details of the bus robberies. It was always the midnight bus which was hit; never the midday one. There was no obvious pattern to the days on which the robberies had occurred, but I printed off the dates anyway. I also found a phone number for the manager of the bus company. After I'd finished up in the records office, I gave him a call, and asked if I could pop straight over to see him.

"It's about time the police sorted this lot out."

For some reason, Mr Grimsdale, the manager of the bus company, was wearing wellingtons with his pin-stripe suit. Maybe, he had a leaking roof? Or just a thing about wellingtons?

"It really isn't good enough. How are we expected to run a public transport system when the passengers are afraid they might be robbed at any moment?"

"I know the police are as keen as you are to clear this up. That's why they've asked me to help."

"No disrespect, but what can you do that the police can't?"

"I'm not sure, but I promise you I'll give it my best."

I could tell he was impressed by the way he snorted.

"What exactly is it you want to see?"

"I'd like to see the rota of drivers for the Washbridge to Candlefield route, if that's possible."

He picked up the phone. "Jeremiah, bring me the WC file would you?"

WC?

He must have noticed my puzzled look. "WC: Washbridge-Candlefield."

"Of course. When you said WC, I thought—never mind."

A quick flick through the paperwork revealed there were in fact five different drivers who drove the route from Washbridge to Candlefield. By crosschecking that rota with the dates of the robberies, it was clear that the same driver had been at the wheel on every occasion. Ricky Keane was now the prime suspect, but I still had no idea how the robberies had taken place.

According to the rota for the current week, he was due to drive the midnight bus again that very night.

"Thank you for your help, Mr Grimsdale."

He snorted what I took to be a goodbye.

***

Once again, at midnight, I found myself at Washbridge bus station, but this time I wasn't waiting for a bus. I was in my car. When the bus displaying the sign *'not in service'* set off, I followed it.

Once the bus had left Washbridge, it stopped only at traffic lights. No one got on or off until it arrived in Candlefield bus station. The burning question was: had there been any robberies? I parked the car and hurried into the bus station. All the passengers leaving the bus seemed perfectly happy. No one had been robbed.

What was going on? I'd been sure Ricky Keane was my man, but he'd driven the bus tonight without incident.

And yet, something about the journey was bugging me. I just couldn't put my finger on what it was.

Chapter 24

"So? Where is she?" Winky demanded when I arrived at the office.

"Where is who?"

"The pretty, young receptionist who has a soft spot for cats."

"I haven't had time to think about that yet. I've been busy."

"Busy? You?" Winky rolled around laughing. "Good one. See, you can be funny when you try."

"I'll have you know I'm very busy at the moment."

"Why don't you let me look after recruiting, then? A good manager knows when to delegate."

"No recruitment agency is going to deal with a cat!"

"I can do it over Skype."

"They can still see you on Skype."

"Not if I put a photo of you in front of the camera. I'll stand behind it and talk to them."

"They'll realise it isn't me when they hear your voice."

"Not necessarily." He took out his smartphone. "Say something."

"Say what?"

"Anything. Just a few words."

"Custard creams are the king of biscuits."

"Don't be ridiculous. Everyone knows that Garibaldi biscuits take the crown."

"Are you honestly trying to compare garibaldis to custard creams?"

"Compare? No. There is no comparison. You're simply wrong."

The cat was a hopeless case. It was pointless to argue

the point.

"Listen." He started to type something into his phone.

"Custard creams are the king of biscuits."

The voice which came from his phone sounded exactly like me.

"How did you do that?"

"I have a voice synthesiser app. I've been recording your voice for some time, so the program could learn it. I think it's done a pretty good job. So, you can leave the recruitment in my paws."

"No! I told you. I'll get it sorted."

"Don't you dare bring back The Buninator!"

The last temp I'd had was Sue Zann or as Winky called her, The Buninator. She scared him to death—she scared me too. I wouldn't be asking *her* back.

"Hello!" A female voice shouted from the outer office. "Anyone home?"

"In here. Come through."

"Sorry. There was no one on reception. Are you Jill Gooder?"

"That's me. How can I help?" Had Winky already been in touch with the recruitment agencies?

"Sorry to call in unannounced. I'm Susan Hall. From The Bugle."

I vaguely remembered Dougal Andrews mentioning something about a new reporter. He'd seemed quite excited about it for some reason. Susan Hall was not what I'd come to expect of reporters who worked at The Bugle.

"I'll be honest with you," I said. "I'm not a fan of The Bugle."

"So I understand. I hope that I'll be able to change your

views over time."

"Take a seat. You've got your work cut out if you want to change my views. That rag of yours will print any old rubbish."

"That's the reason I've been brought in by the new management. They want to change the image of The Bugle."

"You have a mammoth task in front of you. What brings you here to see me?"

"It's obvious that you've played a major part in solving several serious crimes in Washbridge. I've read a number of articles which feature you, including the one about the so-called 'animal' serial killer."

"That's a prime example of The Bugle's tactics. There never was a serial killer. It was pure sensationalism. Is Dougal Andrews still at the paper?"

"For now, yes."

"I should tell you that he and I are not on good terms. He stitched me up with an article on the Washbridge Police. He promised it wouldn't be a hatchet job, and that he'd let me see it before it was published. It *was* a hatchet job, and he *didn't* let me see it. Then, more recently, he accused me of being involved with slavery."

Susan smiled for the first time. "I don't blame you for being upset about that."

"So, what exactly do you hope to achieve?"

"I want to transform The Bugle into a serious newspaper. We should be pursuing the big stories, not frivolous, sensational ones. I want to work *with* the police and people like yourself, not *against* you. I want The Bugle to help make Washbridge a safer place."

"And to pick up a few awards along the way?"

"Sure, but only if they're deserved. I don't want to put my name to articles like the one Dougal Andrews is working on right now, for example. Zombies? Whatever next?"

"Zombies?"

"Ridiculous, I know, but that's what I'm up against. Anyway, Jill, I won't take up any more of your time. I just wanted to introduce myself. I hope we'll be able to work together."

I shook her hand. She was certainly a lot more impressive than any of the other reporters I'd met from The Bugle, but that wasn't saying much.

"Oh, by the way," she said, as she was making her way to the door. "I don't suppose you know of any flat-shares going, do you? I've been living out of a suitcase for ages, in a grotty hotel on the outskirts of town."

"Sorry, I don't. But good luck with the new job."

She was certainly going to need it.

***

Winky was driving me insane. He kept pestering me to find a new receptionist; one who met his exacting requirements. To escape his constant nagging, I magicked myself to the Candlefield bus station.

"You again." Mr Grimsdale greeted me with his usual happy smile. At least today he wasn't wearing wellingtons with his pin-striped suit. Instead, he was sporting open-toe sandals. "I'm still waiting for someone to catch the thief."

"I'm working on it. Do you keep a record of the departure and arrival times of the buses?"

"Of course."

"Could I see them?"

"How is that going to help?"

"Humour me, please."

He grunted a couple of times, but did eventually let me see the records I requested. Within a few minutes, one thing was blatantly obvious. The buses that had been involved with the robberies had all taken about fifteen minutes longer to complete the journey than the buses where no robbery had taken place.

And, I thought I knew why.

***

I'd called Amber in the hope that she could arrange for me to meet with William. As it turned out, he was with her; they were both at the dentist. I said I'd meet them back at Cuppy C.

Twenty minutes after I arrived there, Amber and William came in. Amber was smiling, but looked a little out of it.

"You look a lot happier than the last time I saw you."

"I feel so much better." She was struggling to speak. "I'm going to rinse my mouth out."

"How is she?" I asked William after she'd gone upstairs.

"A lot better. She's still a bit groggy at the moment, but the pain has gone—that's the main thing. Amber said you wanted a word with me?"

"That's right. The other day, you mentioned you used to go on the bus between Candlefield and Washbridge?"

"Yes, but that's a long time ago."

"Didn't you say something about it going on the old route in those days?"

"Yes, that was before they built the more direct route. The old road was longer; it used to meander through the countryside."

"Is the old road still there?"

"Yes, but hardly anyone uses it."

"Do you think you could tell me how to find it?"

"Sure." He took out a small notebook, and began to draw a simple map.

"William!" Amber called. "I think I'm going to have a lie down. Could you bring me a drink, and something to eat—something soft?"

"Sure. I'll be straight up."

William passed me the sketch. "What do you think she would like to eat?"

"Soup? Maybe some fruit—bananas are soft."

"She won't thank me for a banana." He grinned. "She said her mouth tasted like bananas from the anaesthetic."

"Bananas?"

"Yeah. It's the Banacane that they use nowadays. It's brilliant stuff. Knocks you out instantly, but when you come around you have a horrible taste of bananas in your mouth." He stood up. "I'll just take her some soup."

***

I wanted to test my theory by following William's map, but to do that I was going to need my car, which was back in Washbridge.

Once I'd collected it, I set out on the same route that the bus had taken, but I kept a lookout for the left turn, which William had drawn on his map. He would have made a great cartographer; the turn-off onto the old road was exactly where he'd drawn it.

I'd been driving along the old road for about two miles when I came to a tunnel.

Bingo! At long last, everything made sense.

I called Mr Grimsdale to ask when Ricky would next be driving the midnight bus from Washbridge.

He snorted something, but then confirmed it would be that very night.

My next call was to Maxine Jewell.

"What do you want, Gooder?"

"If you ever decide to quit the force, Maxine, you should seriously consider opening a charm school."

"Cut the wisecracks. I'm busy."

"I need you to meet me at Candlefield bus station tonight in time for when the midnight bus arrives."

"I've had just about enough of your wild goose chases."

"Just do it, Maxine. If I don't deliver this time, I'll drop the case."

"You won't need to drop it; I'll kick you off it."

"Fair enough. I need you to send two of your people to another location too."

"You really are pushing your luck. Where?"

I met up with Maxine Jewell and three police officers at the Candlefield bus station just before one in the morning. The bus from Washbridge was due at any moment.

"What's this all about?" Maxine demanded.

"Just wait and see."

Before she could ask again, the bus arrived. When the passengers stepped off, they were all complaining that they'd had their valuables stolen. I stepped onto the bus and grabbed the driver's rucksack.

"Hey! Give me that back!" He chased after me, desperately trying to grab it.

"I think you'll want to see this, Maxine."

I opened the rucksack, and inside, just as I'd suspected, was a gas mask. Maxine looked confused.

"This is your man, Maxine. Arrest him."

"And charge him with what?"

"Robbery, of course."

"Keep a hold of him," she barked at one of the police officers. "You!" She grabbed my arm. "Come with me."

Only when we were out of earshot of the other officers, did she release my arm.

"This had better be good, Gooder."

"Good, Gooder? I like it!"

"You're trying my patience."

"He and his co-conspirator have been using Banacane to knock the passengers out."

"What? How can you know that?"

"When I travelled on the bus, I fell asleep. I never do that when I'm on a case."

"Says you."

"For hours afterwards, I had a horrible taste in my mouth—just like bananas. It was the after-effect of the Banacane. That's why he has the gas mask."

"But where are the stolen goods? And how did he feed the gas into the bus?"

"He's been taking the old road. If you've done what I asked you to, and put your men at the tunnel on that road, they will no doubt have apprehended his partner, and retrieved the stolen goods by now. They'll probably have found the gas cylinders too."

"Stay there for a minute while I check." Maxine moved

a few feet away, and then made a call on her radio.

"Well?" I said when she returned.

"Yes. They've arrested a man."

"And the stolen goods?"

"They have those too. And they've found the gas cylinders and piping."

"This is where you say thank you."

"How did you know he'd been taking the old road?"

"When I took the bus, I was just about to answer a phone call when I lost the signal. It was because we'd stopped in a tunnel. The next thing I knew I was waking up in this bus station. When I followed the bus in my car I knew something was different about the journey, but it took me a while to figure out what it was. Then it came to me—we didn't go through a tunnel. He must have suspected he was being followed that day, so took the regular route. The log times for the buses on which the robberies took place show a slightly longer journey because they took the old road. He and his co-conspirator piped gas into the bus while it was stationary in the tunnel, and then robbed the passengers while they were out of it. His partner took their swag off the bus while Ricky continued on his journey."

"Take him to the station!" She shouted to the police officers. Then almost as an afterthought, she turned back to me. "Thanks."

"Sorry. I didn't catch that."

Chapter 25

The next day, I still couldn't believe I'd actually got a 'Thanks' from Maxine Jewell. Wonders would never cease. I felt like celebrating. Mad had been pestering me to have a night out ever since she'd returned to Washbridge, so I called her, and said I was up for it if she was. Mad was always up for it—I should have known. We arranged to meet that night.

But first, there was something else I needed to do.

I'd had something on my mind ever since my brief meeting with my father. I needed to talk it through with someone otherwise I'd burst. And it had to be someone who could look at it dispassionately, so definitely not family.

I'd called Daze and asked her if she could spare me a few minutes. She said she could, but that she was working, and that I should meet her at a small, private airfield to the south of Washbridge. I readily agreed—I desperately needed to get this thing off my chest.

When I arrived there, it was deserted except for a couple of mechanics working on a small executive jet. They didn't take any notice of me as I drove through the gates, parked, and then waited near the airstrip—just as Daze had instructed.

I was a few minutes early, and there was no sign of her yet. Then, I heard a noise; a small light aircraft was headed towards the airfield. I thought at first it was coming in to land, but then I saw someone leap out of the plane. I was mesmerised as I watched the skydiver plummet towards the ground. When the canopy finally opened, I could see that it wasn't one person; it was a piggy-backed instructor and pupil.

Moments later, they made a perfect landing only a few yards away from where I was standing. The instructor was none other than Daze. The pupil uncoupled herself, thanked Daze, and then headed towards the main building.

"I take it this is your new job?" I was constantly amazed at Daze's versatility.

"Yeah, but to be honest, it's a bit boring."

"Boring? Skydiving?"

"There's lots of hanging around. It's not as exciting as you might think. Have you ever tried it, Jill?"

"No, and I don't intend to. Are you working on a case?"

"Yeah. We're after a gang of wizards. We've had a tip-off they've been using this airstrip to bring in Whizzbang."

"What's that?"

"It's a type of confectionery made in Candlefield, but for some reason it has an inebriating effect on humans. It's almost the equivalent of four beers."

"And they're smuggling it in?"

"That's right. So Blaze and I are working undercover."

"Where is Blaze?"

"He's working as a skydiving instructor too. He'll be on the next trip."

"But surely he's too small."

"You'd be surprised. He's okay with some of the smaller ladies."

"I'll take your word for it."

"Anyway, why did you want to see me, Jill?"

"You're probably going to think I'm crazy but—" I hesitated.

"Go on."

"I met with my birth father recently."

"I'd heard he was back. I didn't think you'd want to see him."

"I didn't, but then I bumped into him when we tried to get the jump on TDO at the Fleur Hotel."

"What was he doing there?"

"That's a good question. He said he'd followed me there to try to persuade me to talk to him."

"You don't sound convinced."

"I don't know what to think. That's why I wanted to talk to you. I've had this crazy idea, and I need someone to tell me that I'm not insane."

"Go on."

"Do you think it's possible that my father is TDO?"

"TDO? Your father?"

"I know it sounds crazy."

"It does a little. What makes you think he might be?"

"Apart from him turning up at the Fleur? Nothing really. But when I sat down and talked to him, the thought just popped into my head. The story goes that he dabbled with black magic, and fell in with a bad crowd."

"It's a long leap from there to him being TDO."

"I know. But I need to be sure. That's why I was wondering."

"Go on."

"There's no way I can follow him. He's bound to spot me, but—"

"You thought I could."

"It's a lot to ask, I know."

"I think you're barking up the wrong tree, but I can start to keep tabs on him as soon as we've finished on this case, if you like?"

"Thanks, Daze. That would be great."

***

Mad and I had arranged to meet inside Bar Ten. I'd been there a couple of times before, but not recently. They'd obviously spent a lot of money on the place since my last visit; it was looking quite splendid.

"Jill, sorry I'm late." Mad was out of breath when she arrived. The contrast between Mad and Madeline was unbelievable. In the daytime Madeline, the librarian, was all prim and proper in her woollen suits, with her hair up in a bun. But Mad, the woman in front of me, was the polar opposite. Her hair was down, and had a mind of its own. She was wearing a skirt which was little more than a belt, and a very low cut top. She looked hot!

"What's that you're drinking?" She pointed to my glass.

"Orange."

"We are *not* drinking orange juice tonight. I plan to get hammered. I want to forget all about Washbridge Public Library. I've had my fill of stamping books, filing books, and logging books on the computer. I need something to numb my brain, and help me to forget about it."

I knew better than to argue with Mad, so we both hit the hard stuff. But, there was no way I could keep pace with her, and I wasn't even going to try. That girl could put drinks away like there was no tomorrow. I had one to every three she had, and yet I felt way tipsier than she seemed to be.

After a couple of hours in Bar Ten, Mad grabbed my arm. "There's a new club not far from the library called

Hunk. Have you heard of it?"

"I can't say I have."

"It's in the old Palace building. You remember the Palace? We used to go there when we were teenagers."

"Yeah, of course I do. What a dump that was."

"It's been completely re-vamped; it opened a couple of weeks ago. Shall we give it a try?"

It wasn't really a question because she was already dragging me out the door.

The building was barely recognisable. Kathy, me, Mad and one or two others used to go to the Palace regularly. I'd met one of my first boyfriends there — another loser. But the building had been transformed. It was all glass and black metal. 'Hunk' was a strange name for a club, but the place looked nice enough.

Wow! It had better be good for that entrance fee.

The décor was amazing, and the music was buzzing. But there was something strange about the place. I just couldn't figure out what it was.

Then it came to me.

There were hardly any men in the club. The few that were there were either working security or behind the bar. What was going on?

We'd only been there for a few minutes when the lights dimmed, and a spotlight lit up the stage.

"Ladies," a voice came over the speakers. "For your pleasure and delight, we are pleased to introduce: *All-Men*."

Suddenly, from behind the curtain, five men rushed onto the stage. *Now*, I understood why the club was called Hunk, and why the audience was predominantly women.

The men went straight into their routine: gyrating, dancing, and then ripping off their shirts to reveal six-packs. The women near the front of the stage screamed and lunged forward. The men obviously knew exactly what they were doing, and managed to stay just out of reach.

"Let's get a bit closer," Mad said.

"No, I'm okay here, thanks."

"Come on, Jill." She grabbed my arm, and pulled me closer to the stage. Just then, the man on the far right of the stage, who was wearing a cowboy hat, caught my eye. Why did he look familiar?

It was Jethro! Aunt Lucy's ex-gardener. I knew he'd produced his own calendar, but I'd no idea he was now working in Washbridge in a male dance troupe. Just wait until I told the twins about this. They'd be green with envy.

Two hours later, and I was out on my feet.

"Come on, Jill. Let's go on to another club," Mad yelled over the music.

"I can't, Mad. I'm sorry. I'm done for."

"Come on. The night's young."

"No, you go ahead. I have to go home. I can't take any more. I'm sorry."

"Okay, then. Are you sure you don't mind if I go off by myself?"

"Of course not. Go and enjoy yourself."

***

Nobody told me it was raining!

When we'd arrived at the club, it had been fine, if a little chilly. Now, the heavens had opened. And did I have a coat? No. Or an umbrella? Of course not.

"Where are all the taxis?" I asked the bored-looking doorman. I'd expected there to be a line of them parked outside the club.

"They don't turn up until just after two a.m. when it's chucking out time. Hardly anyone leaves before then. Why are you going home so early? Had too much to drink?"

"No. I'm perfectly sober, thank you very much." I hiccupped.

He grinned. "If you say so."

I was. Well not entirely sober, but I knew my limit, and had switched back onto orange juice much to Mad's disgust. I was just the right side of 'merry'.

"Where will I get a taxi?"

"They're all down on the high street at this time of night. Most of the late night bars turn out about now."

By the time I made it to the high street, I would have looked like a drowned rat.

"Do you have a phone number I can call?"

"There's two or three next to the payphone." He pointed. "But you're unlikely to get one any quicker. There are plenty of fares for them on the high street without having to come out of their way. Why don't you go back inside until the show's over? Those overpaid narcissists have another set to do yet."

"I take it you're not a fan of All-Men?"

"All-Men?" He laughed. "They should be prosecuted under the Trade Description Act. None of them would last five minutes in the ring with me."

"You're a boxer, then?"

It was a stupid question. He hadn't got his broken nose and cauliflower ears from an origami class.

"I could have been a contender."

Someone had been watching too many movies.

What to do? Suffer another hour in Hunk by myself? Mad had already shot off. Or get soaked to the skin?

"Jill!"

A car had pulled up in front of the club.

"Jill, come on! I'll give you a lift."

It was Drake.

"Looks like your luck's in," the boxer said, as I hurried to the car.

"Jump in!"

I dived into the passenger seat.

"Horrible weather." Drake smiled.

"Where did you come from?" I was mighty pleased to see him, but couldn't work out how he'd turned up out of the blue like that.

"I've been at a business function; it overran a little."

"It must have done."

"It's lucky I spotted you as I was driving past."

"What was the function? It must have been good to keep you out this late."

"Trust me, it wasn't. I'd been trying to get away for the last two hours."

By the time Drake pulled up outside my block of flats, the rain had stopped.

"Thanks for the lift. You saved me from a soaking."

"Do you want me to walk you in?"

"No, I'll be fine from here. Thanks again."

I waved him off and then made my way inside. What a spot of luck that he happened to be passing.

It was only when I got inside my flat that a thought occurred to me: How had Drake known where I lived?

The Susan Hall Mysteries:
Whoops! Our New Flatmate Is A Human.
Whoops! All The Money Went Missing.
Whoops! There's A Canary In My Coffee
See web site for availability.

AUTHOR'S WEB SITE
http:www.AdeleAbbott.com

FACEBOOK
http://www.facebook.com/AdeleAbbottAuthor

MAILING LIST
(new release notifications only)
http:/AdeleAbbott.com/adele/new-releases/

MM July, 2017

MB
Sept 117

MAR - - 2020 LN

BW
AUG - - 2022

49865608R00147

Made in the USA
San Bernardino, CA
06 June 2017